PENGUIN BOO

SOMEWHERE

Jon Robinson was born in Middlesex in 1983. When he's not writing, he works for a charity in central London. Find out more about Jon at:
www.facebook.com/jonrobinsonbooks

Books by Jon Robinson

NOWHERE

ANYWHERE

SOMEWHERE

SOME WHERE

JON ROBINSON

PENGUIN BOOKS

PENGUIN BOOKS

UK I USA I Canada I Ireland I Australia
India I New Zealand I South Africa

Penguin Books is part of the Penguin Random House group of companies
whose addresses can be found at global.penguinrandomhouse.com.

First published 2015
001

Text copyright © Jon Robinson, 2015

The moral right of the author has been asserted

Set in 10.5/15.5 pt Sabon LT Std
Typeset by Jouve (UK), Milton Keynes
Printed in Great Britain by Clays Ltd, St Ives plc

A CIP catalogue record for this book is available from the British Library

ISBN: 978–0–141–34659–5

www.greenpenguin.co.uk

Penguin Random House is committed to a
sustainable future for our business, our readers
and our planet. This book is made from Forest
Stewardship Council® certified paper.

To my readers
Thank you for joining me on this journey

Prologue

A snowstorm lashed at the concrete walls of the prison, rendering the grey stone white. Hidden by acres of surrounding woodland, the building was almost invisible at the best of times. *Then again, that's the whole point*, Henry thought, sitting against the wall of the underground cell. His white beard was flecked with blood from wounds inflicted by the guards when they'd caught him, when he'd been helping Jes and Ryan escape.

Luthan won't just leave me here, he thought. He was sure the Guild would be doing everything they could to free him.

He looked up as the sound of footsteps came down the corridor.

The door opened and Susannah, the teacher, stepped inside.

'Have you come to gloat?' Henry said.

'Felix is dead,' she said abruptly. 'And Stephen Nover has taken control of the Pledge. He's insane ...' She paused, looking around as if someone might overhear.

'Never mind. That's not the only reason I came here. Something's *happening* to the children. I need your help.'

Henry watched her carefully and nodded.

Susannah looked over her shoulder at the door. 'Come in,' she said.

A small frail-looking boy with pale skin entered. His nose was flecked with dried blood.

'He's passed out a couple of times,' Susannah said. 'He's been getting quite confused.'

'I see.'

'Do you want to examine him or –'

'I've seen enough,' Henry said.

'Very well.' Susannah called to the guard, who appeared at the door. 'Take this inmate back to his cell.'

The guard nodded and beckoned to the boy, who quickly left. As soon as their footsteps had disappeared, Henry sighed deeply and looked at Susannah, before saying, 'The Ability is being overused. It's making them sick. When reality is manipulated on such a scale, like you're doing here, it causes the brain to just . . .' Henry snapped his fingers.

'What does that mean?' Susannah asked. 'What will happen?'

'The nosebleeds will get worse. So will the blackouts until he's either lost his mind completely . . . or he just doesn't wake up. And not just the children here. My people too. The escaped inmates.' He stopped and slowly shook his head. 'It'll kill them all.'

Susannah said nothing for a few moments. 'Is there any way of stopping it?'

'End the project,' Henry said. 'At once. Set them free.'

'There's nothing I can do,' she said. 'If I disobey Stephen, he'll just get someone else to take my place. He won't let it end –'

Henry narrowed his eyes. '*We* discovered the Ability, Susannah, all those years ago ... and *you* let it fall into the wrong hands ... You gave it to these psychopaths and now we're all in danger: you, me, the country itself. The children –'

'I know!' she hissed, exasperated. 'But it's *out* of my hands now. I'm just as much of a prisoner as you are.'

Before he could answer, she turned and slammed the door shut.

Henry leant his head back against the wall and closed his eyes.

1

A crow flew on to a lamp post and croaked as a car hurtled round the corner, its speakers blaring. The gust of wind blew a plastic bag on to the snow-covered grass. From the outside, the Guild's building looked like a decrepit block of flats in a south London estate: the last place anyone would expect to find a training school for those who could manipulate reality itself. The only indication was the heavy security gate that barred the front entrance to the building.

Inside the dining room, Luthan, the acting leader of the Guild, studied the group assembled round the table as they ate lunch. A stocky bald man in his early forties with deep-set wrinkles around his eyes, he possessed the intensity of someone who was relishing his opportunity to take charge.

On his right was Elsa, the youngest: small, scrawny, with freckles and frizzy brown hair. The most innocent of the escaped inmates. *The most naive*, he corrected himself silently. *A potential hazard*. Jes, an attractive red-haired girl, was sitting beside her and indignantly prodding her lunch. She seemed to be growing more and more angry, but he admired her no-nonsense attitude. If her skill increased, she might some day make a fine member. Ryan, next to her, obviously had feelings for her – only a fool could not see it. But his aggression would need to be kept under control, or he might be a problem.

Luthan then looked over at Julian, a slim boy with dark hair and pointed elfin features. He'd heard tales of how he was clever, but a traitor. Luthan liked to think anyone could change, but, if not, Julian might need to go; the Guild couldn't risk someone like that among its ranks. But, despite his manipulative streak, Julian seemed less keen on altering reality than the others, to the point of self-righteousness. At the other end of the spectrum was Harlan, a tall, quiet Indian boy who kept himself guarded. He was desperate to join them. Maybe a little too desperate. Luthan noticed he'd been spending an increasing amount of time using the Ability. It seemed like it was starting to become an obsession.

'Henry is a prisoner in Nowhere,' said Luthan from the head of the dining table, 'and the Pledge's project is still underway. They might think they're saving the country, but we all know what this is really about ... power. And *money*.' Luthan paused, as the group took in his words. 'As long as *they* are around,' he continued, 'none of *you* will ever be safe.'

'Neither are the rest of us now they know the Guild exists,' said Pyra resentfully.

She was in her early twenties, wearing a leather jacket and tattered jeans. Her black hair was short and spiky and fell across one eye. Pyra had joined the Guild at a young age, and she too had taken a while to fit in. Now she was one of the most valuable members of the team. Quick, fearless. Willing to do whatever it took.

Ryan was slouched in his chair with his hood up and his hands in his pockets. He had barely touched his food.

'What do you think, Ryan?' said Luthan.

Ryan gave a feeble shrug. 'Dunno.'

'This is *your* future too,' said Luthan. 'Giving it some thought might not be such a bad idea.'

'Look, mate, I don't know! I don't know what to say. Yeah, they're all scumbags. Stephen's a nutter . . .'

Luthan leant forward and locked his fingers together. 'The inmates in Nowhere are forced to watch films containing subliminal messages: a way to harness the Ability without them realizing –'

'To make things happen,' Jes interrupted. 'We know. We were there, remember?'

'We need to stop the project,' Luthan said. 'But to do that we need to get inside.'

'There's a tunnel in the yard,' Harlan said. '*Was* a tunnel. I'm sure it's been blocked up by now.'

'All of you are quite sure there's no other way in?'

The group shook their heads. 'Place is like a fort,' said Ryan.

'And to get into a fort, you need an army,' Julian

offered. 'And you don't have one. You've only got us. Sorry to break it to you, but Henry's not getting out of there. And you're not getting in.'

Half an hour later, everyone had finished eating and went their separate ways, without resolution. After some moments sitting alone, Luthan went into the corridor. When he was certain there was no one around, he walked over to a door in the middle of the corridor and knelt down, removing a small key from a secret compartment in the wooden skirting-board.

He unlocked and opened the door and entered. In the darkness Luthan could just make out the faintest hint of a shape, silhouetted against the wall. 'Hang on in there,' he said. 'I'm doing everything I can to stop it.'

With that, Luthan stepped back outside, locked the door and put the key back inside the panel.

2

After their meal, Jes and Elsa went up on to the roof of the Guild's building to practise the most basic test given to trainee members: manipulating a coin to land on its side.

'It's not working,' Jes said after yet another failed attempt. She hadn't kept count, thankfully. It would've only depressed her.

She looked over at Elsa, who was enveloped in Pyra's leather jacket. 'If I can't even do this, what good will I be trying to get revenge on the Pledge?'

'Revenge?' Elsa looked confused. 'I thought we were just supposed to be stopping the project and freeing the inmates . . .'

That too, Jes thought. But, after everything they had been put through, revenge was the more attractive option. She flipped the coin in the air and closed her eyes. It hit the roof, rolled slightly and fell flat.

'You remind me of me,' said Elsa. 'I never thought I'd make it work either!'

She ran over to the roof edge and peered over. On the

pavement below an elderly balloon seller, on his way to a children's party, was struggling to control his colourful jumble of inflatables.

'I'm going to get myself one of those balloons! Just watch.' Elsa shut her eyes and whispered 'blue elephant', her locus, over and over to help her concentrate.

Jes sighed and folded her arms sceptically. A moment later, a cloud drifted from in front of the sun, causing the misty winter light to glimmer on the surface of the road. A driver missed the traffic light that had just turned red. His car sped through the junction and almost collided with an oncoming vehicle, which in turn careered on to the pavement.

The old man turned and jumped backwards, momentarily letting go of his balloons. He reached up, managing to grasp all of the strings but one. A balloon floated up on a gust of air towards the Guild's tower block.

Elsa pointed at the balloon, grinning, as it slunk silkily upward. 'I made that happen. It's just practice!'

Jes smiled but said nothing. She wasn't used to being left behind; she had always been popular and socially and academically gifted. Exams came easily to her. She had often felt a pang of guilt around results time, when her friends, who worked far harder than she did, ended up with less to show for it than her. Naturally talented, her parents and teachers had said.

Except now.

'I've been thinking about what happened in the opera house,' said Elsa.

Jes nodded. 'I just don't know what Alyn was thinking. I mean, he was there – with Felix. The leader of the Pledge . . . the people who put us there! Why?'

'People change, right?'

'That's what scares me,' Jes said.

She too had changed. She had never been angry – far from it – but ever since they had been taken, the anger had been growing quietly inside her. She had spent months staring at the same grey walls, the same forest shutting them off from the rest of the world, the same shadow of iron bars falling across her while she slept. She wasn't a bad person – was she? Back home, they'd told her how brilliant she was, and she had lived up to it. But in the prison she'd been told something else: that she was vicious, violent. *Dangerous*.

'Things aren't ever going to be the same, are they?' she said, gazing as the clouds slipped back across the sun.

Elsa looked at her questioningly.

Jes went on. 'With us, I mean. We tried to tell everyone in the opera house about the Pledge but no one believed us – they all just thought we were crazy. We're never going back. This is it now. Us versus *them*. Even if we get home, things will never be the same as they were. If you think about it like that, I guess you could say the Pledge has *won*.'

Elsa tried to smile, but it looked more like a grimace.

'We know why they put us there. But we're still prisoners, aren't we? Until they're all gone, we'll never be safe.' Jes looked at Elsa for a response. But Elsa was unscrewing a yellow bottle of children's bubbles. She dipped the plastic stick inside, raised it to her mouth and blew. 'You listening, Elsa?'

'Huh?'

A web of quivering bubbles, gilded with oily blue and green, wobbled slowly across the white sky.

'Bubbles,' Jes said, raising an eyebrow. '*Really . . .*'

Elsa beamed. 'Yup, Harlan bought me them from the shop.' She dipped the stick back in and blew again. 'I told him I always liked to imagine there's a problem inside each of those bubbles and they're just blowing away!' She looked over her shoulder at Jes.

Jes got up and went and sat beside Elsa on the roof edge. She took the plastic stick from her and blew, then laughed.

'See?' Elsa said.

'You're easily amused,' Jes said with a look that might have been envy.

Elsa seemed momentarily embarrassed.

'No, no. It's a good thing,' Jes said. 'Here, let me have another go.'

The two girls sat on the roof side by side, laughing at the bubbles while everything around them was beginning to fall apart.

3

'So that's really what it's all about for you, Stephen?' said Antonia, the third-ranking member of the Pledge. 'Money?'

Stephen Nover, the twenty-one-year-old billionaire and new leader of the Pledge, leant back in his chair, his Italian designer shoes resting on the desk's edge. Beneath them was a newspaper showing a picture of the now-deceased Felix on the front page. To his left sat Lord Blythe, a barrel-shaped aristocrat and the second-wealthiest man in the country.

'Yes, Antonia,' he answered coolly. 'Money. What else would it be about? Truth? Justice? Equality?' He tipped his head back. 'Ha! Those are all just words. *Meaningless* words. Intangible. But money –' he gazed out of the window, a broad smile creeping across his face – 'money is real, Antonia. Money is the only thing it's *ever* been about!'

'*Semper ad meliora*,' Antonia said coldly. The disdain was clear on her face. 'It means "ever towards better things". That's what we agreed, Stephen.'

'Yes, when Felix was in charge. And look where that got him!' He threw his head back, giggling with delight. His movements were floppy and exaggerated, like a child who had not yet mastered control of his limbs.

Antonia watched him silently and started fiddling with her diamond bracelet. 'There are still six escaped inmates, and this other group – the Guild – who seem to be helping them.'

Blythe scratched his grey moustache. 'And we have their leader – this Henry fellow, don't we? They'll be coming to *us*. And we'll be ready for them!'

'I've already made plans at the prison,' Stephen said. 'If Susannah Dion is to be trusted, some of my changes will be coming into effect very soon . . .'

Stephen clasped his hands behind his head, smirking. The solution seemed simple: there were just too many people fighting over too few resources.

'And if she *isn't* to be trusted?' said Blythe.

Stephen opened his mouth to speak, but stopped. It was true, Susannah had seemed less than thrilled with his plans. If she developed a conscience now, it would be a terrible inconvenience. 'I'll have someone watch over her,' he said, pondering. 'Just to be on the safe side.'

'*My* concern is Felix's adviser,' Antonia said. 'This Emmanuel character. After what he did to Felix . . .'

'Quite! I've never trusted him either,' said Blythe, burping into his hand. 'Always thought there was something strange about him. I told Felix I thought he might be using us all for his own purposes, but the old boy didn't listen.'

Stephen put a hand to his chin. 'I'm not going to do anything rash just yet. But leave Emmanuel to me. I'm sure I'll be able to make him see my point of view.'

'Felix tried that,' Blythe answered. 'Didn't end well, did it?'

As much as it pained Stephen to accept that the others were right, Emmanuel was a growing concern, a dangerous enigma without an obvious motive.

'If it comes to it, Emmanuel will have to be removed,' Stephen answered, although he suspected that it might be a little more difficult than that.

4

'This way,' Emmanuel said, holding a lantern in front of him.

Dressed formally in a grey suit, his tidy black hair and calm demeanour gave no clue as to his intentions; he was a blank canvas, a seemingly ordinary man, the kind of man you might pass on the street and give no further thought to. Still, Alyn detected something cold yet strangely compelling about him.

Something dangerous.

'You can stay here with me,' Emmanuel continued. 'This is a safe place, somewhere the Pledge will never find you.'

Alyn followed him through a narrow arch, brushing his dark fringe out of his eyes.

Everything had descended into chaos last night at the opera house. Felix had planned to vote Stephen out of the Pledge, but Stephen had secretly been using Nowhere to cause Felix's fortune to crash. That was the last time Alyn had seen Felix alive. He paused and leant against the wall. His friends had been there too: Ryan, Harlan,

Elsa, Julian . . . Jes. And he'd saved them. Alyn shut his eyes, but the scene repeated itself again and again: the brass chandelier plummeting down on to Stephen's men, the screams and the shattering of bones . . .

'Come on,' Emmanuel said over his shoulder.

Alyn walked after him in silence and soon they entered a large chilly room. The wind howled through the crumbling stone. Emmanuel placed the lantern on a hook and slowly the darkness peeled away, revealing a derelict church.

Alyn walked between the rows of pews, shivering. Strange, sinister-looking glyphs were etched on the walls in chalk, the graffiti of a deranged and dedicated mind. A few leather-bound books were scattered on a broken chair in a corner at the front. Alyn lifted one up.

'You don't have much to say,' said Emmanuel, watching Alyn carefully.

'I'm more interested in what *you* have to say,' he answered. 'I want to know who you are. I want to know how to destroy the Pledge. I don't care what it takes. I want them gone so me and my friends can get back to our lives. I want to know when all of this is going to end.'

Emmanuel held a candle against the lantern flame until it took light. 'It will end as soon as I take control of the project – of *Nowhere*.'

A creeping suspicion filled Alyn. 'Why do *you* want control of it?'

'To start a revolution. To tear down everything, to overthrow our rulers so we can start again. So we can start anew from the ashes. It's what everyone wants, Alyn. Haven't you noticed the anger? The hatred simmering beneath the surface?' Emmanuel's voice was quiet but cold. 'I'm going to use Nowhere to cause a blackout in the city. It's the only way the revolution can begin. In the darkness.'

Alyn looked at Emmanuel, unable to muster any words.

'Society is a work in progress,' Emmanuel went on, 'and progress is the work of a blind sculptor. Once in a while it needs a helping hand.'

Alyn watched him closely. 'That's what the Pledge says.'

'The Pledge is only concerned with keeping things as they are, so *they* can prosper. A true revolution would mean they too are overthrown. The Pledge was necessary. The project would have never got underway without the funds and influence of the wealthiest.'

And you were the one pulling the strings all along, Alyn thought. 'So that means you want to get rid of them?'

Emmanuel lit another candle and placed it on the far wall.

'Soon, Alyn. But I have another concern. A group who call themselves the Guild.'

A surge of panic rose in Alyn's chest. 'Never heard of them,' he lied, and walked over to the wall. There was a mound of crinkled and cracked leaves, and weeds poked through the stone.

Emmanuel gave him a piercing look. 'They're planning to free everyone from the prison and expose the Pledge. But I can't allow this to happen before my own plans are realized. Help me, Alyn, and you will never need worry about the Pledge ever again. And you and your friends will be free.'

'What if I say no?'

Emmanuel smiled and walked away. 'Rest now. And think carefully, Alyn.'

Alyn waited until Emmanuel was gone and lay down on the nearest pew, looking up at the stained and crumbling ceiling. Finally there was someone else who wanted to destroy the Pledge, the group who had kidnapped him and his friends – and many others – imprisoning them in Nowhere. As long as the Pledge was still around, none of them were safe. But could Emmanuel be trusted?

'The lesser of two evils,' he murmured, and closed his eyes.

5

Harlan stood in the dingy, noisy amusement arcade a short distance from the Guild's headquarters. A crowd of people gathered around him as he fed another coin into the flashing machine.

'Hey, you wanna give me some of that luck?' said an overweight man beside him, laughing.

'Me too,' said another. 'I've never seen anyone do this to a machine. The damn thing must be broken . . .'

'It ain't broken, unless every machine in the place is. This is the *third* machine I've seen this kid wipe out in half an hour.'

The other pair murmured and ran to the surrounding machines, fumbling in their pockets for coins.

Harlan shrugged. 'Just one of those days,' he said humbly.

He jabbed the red button and closed his eyes, willing the jackpot. Unlike his friends, Harlan didn't need a locus – a word or gesture or tool to help him concentrate. It was being in the prison, with nothing more than a silver coin, where he had learned how to manipulate coincidence, to change the world.

As a clatter of warm coins cascaded into the tray, the young man beside him burst into laughter, patting Harlan enthusiastically on the back.

Harlan grinned. It wasn't even so much the money that excited him, but the sense of winning, the feeling that he had broken the rules.

'Hang on a minute, I know you,' the young man said suddenly, frowning as he looked closely at Harlan. 'You're that missing teenager. I saw you on the news. I thought you looked familiar.'

Harlan froze. 'You're mistaken,' he answered, shovelling the money into the makeshift pouch he'd made with his jumper.

'Hey, that's right,' said the older man, who had given up on a machine behind the pair. 'I've seen you too. What happened, you run away or something?'

'I – I don't know what you're talking about,' Harlan said, and walked away anxiously.

6

Ryan pulled his hood over his head and hurried down the stairwell. He screwed up his face as he entered the musty hallway, treading on litter and leaves, and unlocked the security gate.

He wondered how Henry was getting on at the prison. It was their fault he'd got caught, after all. He thought back to being there with Jes in those tunnels. At least now he had a clean bed and food and warmth, but he couldn't help but think how great it had been then, just him and her together.

The Guild said that the Ability could make things happen, as long as you could imagine them; he still wasn't sure he believed it. But one thing he could imagine was Jes falling helplessly in love with him. It was all he'd thought about since he'd met her.

Pyra was furious with him when he'd mentioned using the Ability to move things on a little with Jes. *Bet she's done the same thing before*, Ryan thought. *Bet they all have*. The Ability was like using a cheat code in a computer game, or so Anton said. Sometimes, when it mattered, you needed to cheat now and then.

'Ryan.'

He glanced up. Luthan was leaning out of the window of a car, pulled up at the kerb.

'What do you want?'

'I'm going on a little errand,' said Luthan. 'Want to come?'

'Dunno. Depends where you're going.'

'The apartment of a dead billionaire,' Luthan answered.

'Go on then,' Ryan said, trying to hide his excitement, and yanked open the door. 'Got nothing better to do.'

They drove in silence to Felix's apartment, Ryan gazing out of the car window.

Luthan parked outside a huge glass-fronted building. 'So you think you're gonna find something here, right?' Ryan asked as the pair left the car and walked towards the main entrance. It was early evening and snowflakes fluttered down around them.

Luthan smiled. 'Right. And it also gives you and me a chance to get to know each other.'

Ryan looked at him sarcastically, then followed him over to the secure glass door at the front, where a security guard was standing. 'Good luck getting in here.'

'We don't need luck.'

Ryan scowled, glancing through the glass at the guard. 'So are we gonna beat him up or –'

'No beating people up.' Luthan shut his eyes. 'You'll be surprised how persuasive the feeling of a full bladder can be.'

Ryan watched as the security guard shuffled uncomfortably and loosened his belt.

'So you're gonna make him p–'

'Wet himself?' Luthan interrupted, and returned his attention to the guard. 'I hope it doesn't come to that.'

The guard looked left and right; when he was quite sure nobody was watching, he turned and ran towards the public toilets.

Ryan shrugged. 'Still reckon we should've beaten him up.'

'The Ability is a gentle art. It's about working *with* the universe. Not against it.' Luthan removed some black gloves from his coat. 'Put these on.'

Ryan pulled on the gloves and the pair entered the building and went straight to the lift. At the penthouse on the top floor they stepped out on to the mahogany floorboards and walked over to another frosted-glass door. Luthan took some pieces of wire from his pocket and slipped them into the lock.

'So what're you looking for?' Ryan asked, leaning against the wall with his hands in his pockets.

'A key, a code, anything that might help us get into the prison and free everyone. It's the only way to end the project.'

Luthan looked up as a security guard emerged suddenly from round the corner.

'Hey!' the guard yelled, reaching for his radio, but before he could say a word Ryan pulled an ibis from his sleeve and fired. A translucent blast streamed out of the barrel, slamming the security guard into the wall. A grin flashed on Ryan's face. He and the others had taken the weapons from the guards shortly after escaping from Nowhere. He still didn't really understand how they worked; it was something to do with a sound wave. But he didn't care. Considering all the recent happenings, Ryan had taken to carrying his ibis wherever he went.

Ryan leant down and swooped the guard's set of keys up from the floor. He tossed them towards Luthan. 'I don't do gentle,' he said.

Luthan smiled and opened the door. 'I'll find somewhere to put our uninvited guest. You start looking.'

Luthan went over to the security guard and dragged him inside.

Ryan looked around at the extravagant interior of white walls and screens and whistled approvingly. He quickly began searching the apartment, looking behind picture frames, inside books and beneath the rug.

'We'll need to hurry,' Luthan said once he had finished securing their prisoner. 'They'll send back-up when they realize they can't get through to him.'

Ryan opened a walk-in wardrobe, stopping to examine an expensive-looking watch on the table. *It must be worth tens of thousands*, he thought, and shoved it in his pocket. *It'll make a nice present for Mum when I get back. An apology for me being gone and everything.*

Fifteen minutes passed quickly. 'Found anything, Ryan?' Luthan called from the next room.

'Nah. Nothing,' Ryan said, making sure the watch was well hidden. 'Nothing at all.'

He had just entered the bedroom and was close to giving up when he noticed something on a glass table beside the window. He picked it up. It was an envelope, with *Alyn* written on the front.

'Wait!' he called. 'I think I've got something.'

Ryan opened the envelope and took out a piece of paper. He read it out to Luthan.

Should anything happen to me, I hope this letter finds you well.

As you know, I formed the Pledge as a force for good: to repair everything that has gone wrong in the last several years and to restore the country to its former glory.

As time passes, I fear that I made a grave error and Nowhere will be used for the wrong reasons: for evil. Should this happen in my absence, Alyn, the project must end and Nowhere must be erased from existence. There will be casualties, but there is no other way.

Each of the Pledge has a key; this is mine. Combine the four Pledge keys and the prison will be destroyed, the prisoners will be released and the project will end.

It is the only way to stop the madness I had a part in making.

James Felix

'Is there a key?' Luthan asked from over Ryan's shoulder.

'Not here,' Ryan said with a sinking sense of disappointment.

'Maybe Alyn already took it.' Luthan looked at his watch. 'Come on, we'd better hurry.'

7

Pyra held her hands a few centimetres from Jes's head. 'If you concentrate hard enough, you can *feel* the Ability,' she said. 'It surrounds people, like a force.'

'Well, can you feel anything yet?' said Jes.

'No. Keep trying.'

Jes breathed deeply and looked out of the window. Outside, birds were perched in the bare trees. It had been snowing through the night, and the snow had turned hard and slick. Jes watched a few people teetering on the pavement below.

Pyra glanced at a metal box with a flashing row of digits. 'The number generator isn't showing any patterns.'

'I was concentrating, I swear.'

'You've tried all the basic tests,' Pyra said. 'You couldn't put out the flame?'

'No. *Ryan* could.'

'Maybe you need to start with something even more basic. How about making the coin land heads up ten times in a row?'

Jes shook her head.

'Five times then. Start small . . .'

Jes shook her head a second time. 'Already tried. Couldn't do that either.'

'Hmm.' Pyra removed her hands. 'Sorry, Jes, but I'm beginning to think that you don't have it.'

'But, wait, they put me through all of this – kidnapping me, making me stay in that place . . . and I don't even have the Ability?'

Pyra shook her head. 'You *might* have had it. At one point. But like anything it can be lost. It's usually caused by some kind of traumatic event.'

Jes was silent for a few moments. *Adler, the chief warden.* On the day of their escape he had surrendered, defenceless. But by then the anger had already consumed her and she'd shot him with the ibis again and again until he had stopped moving.

I took a man's life. Everything had changed from then on. She felt different, older. Like she had lost something.

'A traumatic event,' she repeated, feeling the blood leave her face and nausea swirling in her stomach.

'You OK?' said Pyra.

Jes nodded. 'Try again,' she said, attempting to change the subject. 'Please. This time I'll concentrate even harder.'

Pyra sighed and held her hands close to Jes's head again.

At that moment Elsa burst into the room, smiling. 'I'm ready to take my test,' she said. 'I'll be a level-two member of the Guild. How cool is that? I'm basically a superhero!'

Jes forced a smile. 'Good for you, Elsa. I'm sure you'll do a great job.'

Elsa beamed. 'Anyway, Luthan says he wants to talk to us. Come on. He says it's important.'

'Now you're all here, we can get started,' said Luthan, as Jes followed Elsa into the dining room. 'There have been some developments. Thanks to a recent discovery, we –'

'Thanks to me,' Ryan interrupted. Jes noticed he was looking at her, smiling.

'Yes. Thanks to you, Ryan, we found a note from Felix.' He paused, making sure they were all watching him. 'To your friend, Alyn.'

There was a murmur from the group at the table.

Jes's eyes went to the floor as she felt the air leave her lungs. He was working with Felix after all. Elsa had been right.

'It seems that each of the Pledge has a key. When all the keys are combined together, the prison will collapse.'

'Literally?'

'That's what Felix's note suggests. It looks like the Pledge wanted the project to last a couple of years before releasing everyone – including all of you – and leave no trace of it ever having been there.'

With Stephen in charge, there's no chance of it ending any time soon, if ever, Jes thought, crossing her arms. She noticed Ryan looking at her across the table and returned his smile.

'The rest of the Guild have left for Nowhere. They're

hoping to find some way to free Henry. That just leaves us,' said Luthan. 'I suggest we split into teams.'

'I'll take Stephen,' Julian declared. 'Preferably alone.'

'Stephen's the most dangerous of them all,' Luthan said. 'I'll take him.'

'But he knows *me*,' Julian said. 'I can draw him out.'

Luthan scrutinized Julian carefully. 'We'll go together,' he said. 'You and I.'

'Harlan, Elsa, you two come with me,' said Pyra. 'We'll go after Antonia, along with Charlie.' Charlie, an Asian man with a silver crucifix dangling against his T-shirt, nodded his agreement.

'Guess that leaves me and you,' Ryan said to Jes, sounding pleased.

'Actually, Ryan, you'll be with me,' Anton said. 'We'll take Blythe.'

'That just leaves me,' said Jes. *Or have you already forgotten me?*

Luthan shared a look with the other members of the Guild before turning to her, but it was Pyra who spoke. 'We don't think you have the Ability, Jes. We think it'd be best if you stayed here for now.'

'So I can't get involved? Is that what you're saying?' Jes felt herself starting to tremble. She balled her hands into fists. 'I've got as much right as the rest of you to get involved! Just because I'm not *special* doesn't mean I can't help you.'

Julian smirked, tapping his mug. 'Jes, another coffee, when you're next getting up.'

'Get your own, Julian. I'm not your slave,' Jes hissed.

'Well, you aren't one of *us*, are you? You might as well have some use around here . . .'

'Hey, shut up, Julian,' Ryan spat. 'Stop being an idiot.'

Harlan turned to Luthan. 'You can't just stop her, guys. After everything we've been through together . . .'

'No, Harlan, maybe he's right,' Jes said bitterly, scowling at Julian. 'Maybe I should just leave. I mean, there's not much point me being here now, is there?'

'Leaving would be a bad idea,' Luthan said. 'Especially while the Pledge still has people looking for you. You can stay with us for as long as you need, Jes.'

Jes nodded, feeling tears welling up. If the rest of the group were being taught to use their amazing 'powers', she could think of nothing worse than having to sit and watch helplessly from the sidelines.

'Besides, my partner doesn't have the Ability either,' Luthan continued. 'And he *is* our leader after all.' There was a pause.

'Henry?' Jes said, surprised. 'You two are . . . a couple?'

Luthan's eyes softened. 'We're a couple.'

'So,' Pyra said. 'Are you staying with us?'

A lump rose in Jes's throat. 'I don't see the point, knowing I'll never be able to do what you guys can do. It doesn't seem fair.' She got to her feet.

'Where are you going?' Elsa said, tugging her sleeve.

'Just want to go for a walk,' said Jes. 'Clear my head.' *Don't need some stupid Ability anyway*, she thought as she passed through the door. After all, it was just cheating.

You've been fine up until now, she reminded herself, swallowing her anger. There'll always be privileged people in the world, people who have it easy. Usually, she thought smugly, they are the ones who never reach their full potential. So this would push her to try harder. She would do just as well – if not better – than any of the others.

'Hey!' Ryan called, running to join her. 'You all right?'

Jes nodded. 'I'm fine, Ryan,' she said, throwing him a smile.

'Just checking,' he said with a shrug. 'Man, sometimes I just wanna punch Julian in his stupid mouth . . .'

Jes looked at him gratefully and felt a flutter in her stomach. She remembered back to when they were in the tunnel, when he had helped her.

'Erm, you're looking at me kinda weird,' he said awkwardly.

'Oh, I –' Jes faltered. 'It's nothing.' With that, she turned and quickly left.

8

'Sir?' said Blythe's elderly butler, tapping gently on the door.

Blythe sat in front of the blaring television in his study, staring at the ornate brass key in his hand.

'*Sir?*' Blythe's butler repeated, raising his voice. 'You wanted to see me.'

Blythe belched loudly. 'Yes, yes. Come in.'

Blythe put the key back inside a wooden box on the arm of his chair. The television screen showed the haggard-looking Prime Minister, who had only just returned to the public eye after a brief holiday abroad.

Blythe laughed. 'Looks a bloody wreck, doesn't he?'

'Indeed,' his butler said. 'What was it you wanted to see me about, sir?'

'Hmm. Oh yes, well, I have some rather bad news.' He paused momentarily. 'Need to keep check of my spending, you see. That villa in Florence needed a tad more work than I thought it would. Ended up paying through the nose.' Blythe chuckled to himself. 'I need to watch my bank balance, so the accountants keep telling me.'

'I'm no longer needed, sir? Is that what you're saying?'

'Not yet! But I'll be considerably reducing your hours. I'm sure you'll cope. Perhaps cut back on the luxuries for a little while. Besides, these things do you good. Build character, as my dear old father used to say.'

Blythe's butler nodded. 'Yes. Yes, sir. But I'll need to take on another job as, with all due respect, sir, I barely make enough as it is . . .'

Blythe picked up a cigar from his ashtray, waving his hand dismissively. He sucked on the cigar and coughed out a plume of smoke. He turned back to the television and, as he did so, knocked the wooden box from the chair. The catch opened and the key slid across the floor.

His butler leant down to pick it up, but Blythe swatted his hand out of the way.

'*I'll* take that,' he said, grabbing it. 'Anyway, try to not let it bother you, old chap. These are difficult times for everyone. Chin up!' He patted his butler hard on the shoulder and settled back in his chair.

9

Alyn sat in the back of the car, watching the city drifting past as snowflakes spilled across the glass.

He reached into his jacket pocket and inspected the key he had taken from Felix as he lay on the ballroom floor two days ago. Maybe it was nothing at all, just a piece of junk, a lucky charm. He unscrewed the shaft of the key and removed the piece of paper.

51.51

What did it mean?

'We're here,' Emmanuel said from the passenger seat.

Alyn slyly slipped the key into the back pocket of his jeans. He left the car and followed Emmanuel and his assistant, a weasel-faced man, towards a warehouse. Its bulk was framed formidably against the grey sky.

Emmanuel turned to Alyn. 'Cities always have the largest influence, which makes them the most fragile. And that's why London will need to fall. Where the Pledge saw a threat, *I* saw an opportunity.'

'For chaos,' Alyn answered. 'You're using Nowhere to cause a blackout.'

'An electromagnetic pulse caused by the subjects in the prison. Everything electrical will be ruined, made useless. People will be lost. Without security, anarchy will quickly follow. We destroy the infrastructure of the city. We attack the government; we burn all of their buildings to the ground.'

Alyn watched him cautiously. 'Who's *we*?'

'Over the past few years, I've been working with some anti-government groups around the country.'

'You mean the same kind of groups that the Pledge were trying to stop?'

Emmanuel didn't need to answer. Alyn had already seen a flicker of confirmation in his face. He felt a growing unease.

'Here we are,' said Emmanuel's assistant, unbolting a padlock on the shuttered doors. There was a hiss nearby as two cats duelled in the swirling snow.

Alyn followed Emmanuel through the doors into the warehouse and instantly noticed a mass of people gathered at the far end, at least seventy, but probably more. The central space was filled with ominous-looking wooden crates covered with tarpaulins. Beside them was an assortment of cheap-looking plastic animal masks: lambs, pigs, bulls and apes.

A map showing the Houses of Parliament on top of one of the crates caught Alyn's eye. He picked it up, but Emmanuel's assistant snatched it out of his hands.

'Looks like a social club for anarchists,' Alyn said, hoping that humour might ease the tension.

'This is where the revolution begins!' Emmanuel's assistant exclaimed, intoxicated by the promise of rebellion. 'This is our fiftieth cell . . . We're going to bring down everything so the country can start again from scratch. Just like we planned. And it's all thanks to you, sir,' he said, looking at Emmanuel. 'You brought us all together. We were directionless before, but under your leadership I know we can succeed.'

'And succeed we shall.'

Emmanuel guided Alyn up a flight of creaking metal stairs and along a walkway, overlooking the rest of the warehouse. Alyn leant against its railing and watched the activity beneath him. One group was shifting a crate from one side of the warehouse to the other, while another group of six sat at a wire-strewn table, intently studying a laptop.

'If you want to get rid of the Pledge,' Alyn said, 'that's fine by me. But I don't want a part of anything else. I mean, you want someone to join you? To do what?'

Emmanuel narrowed his eyes. 'I see a lot of potential in you, Alyn. I look at you and I see a young man who reminds me of myself.'

'You're wrong.'

'Your grasp of the Ability is second only to mine, Alyn. On the same side, we'll be undefeatable.'

'You mean you want to use me to get rid of the Guild.' Alyn shook his head. 'No. No, Emmanuel. I won't do it.'

He started to walk away, but Emmanuel called after him. 'When I eventually destroy the Guild, Alyn, your friends will be there. And if you refuse me I'll destroy them too. All of them.'

Alyn stopped and turned round slowly. His heart was racing, and sound seemed muffled in his ears.

'Are you threatening to kill my friends?'

Emmanuel walked towards Alyn. 'Not *just* your friends.'

He pushed open a door on the upper level. 'Look inside,' he said.

Alyn peered cautiously into the room. There was a man on the floor, gagged and tied up with rope. He gasped, taking a step back. 'Dad?'

His father, unshaven and bleary-eyed, tried to respond but his voice was muffled.

Alyn rushed over, knelt down beside him and lifted the gag. 'Dad, are you all right? Did he hurt you?'

'He's a maniac!' his father shouted, his eyes wide. 'That bloke over there, he's out of his mind! He kidnapped me!'

'Think of this as an incentive, Alyn,' Emmanuel said. 'Do what I ask of you, and your father, and your friends, will be unharmed.'

'You're sick,' Alyn whispered. He put a hand on his father's shoulder and looked up at Emmanuel with hatred clouding his eyes.

'I want you to bring me the leader of the Guild, Alyn. His name is Luthan.' Emmanuel tossed a photograph at

Alyn. It was a black-and-white security image showing a bald man in a tuxedo. Alyn recognized him from the opera house.

'So you can kill him?' Alyn hissed. 'Get him yourself.'

'You can get much closer to him than I can, Alyn,' Emmanuel said. 'Do it. Or your friends, your father . . . all of them will suffer.' He looked over his shoulder at the masked figures who had appeared behind him. 'Take him away.'

With that, two of Emmanuel's followers grabbed Alyn under his arms and dragged him out of the room.

'Alyn!' his father shouted. 'Please, Alyn, you have to help me! Don't leave me here! He'll kill me!'

His cries quickly faded, as Alyn was hauled along the walkway, struggling and wrestling with his captors.

10

Snow was fluttering silently outside the Guild's tower block, coating the road beneath. Every few minutes a car crawled past, tracing two black lines in the tarmac.

Elsa sat with Harlan and Pyra, staring at a photograph. It showed a lavish mansion with domed towers bearing a gold-plated spike, similar to ones Elsa had seen in pictures of Russia.

She felt a reluctant admiration for the mansion's owner, Antonia Black. After all, if *she* was ever a billionaire, she planned on having a palace made of crystal, perhaps with trained penguins to serve as her butlers.

'Pretty awesome,' she intoned. 'And I thought this place was cool . . .'

Harlan took the next photograph and examined it. 'Is that a hedge maze?'

'Yup,' said Pyra.

'I can't believe anyone didn't realize she was a supervillain sooner,' Harlan mumbled. 'I mean, have you ever seen a *normal* person with a hedge maze?'

'Jealous, Harlan?'

He shrugged. 'A little.'

'The house is about two hours away,' Pyra said, playing absentmindedly with her domino locus. 'It's surrounded by forty acres of land. Reckon we should probably park up in one of the fields and camp out, then head there first thing.'

'Camp out?' Elsa protested. 'In the middle of winter?' The thought made her shiver.

Harlan pushed the photograph back towards Pyra. 'What made you guys change your tune about us helping? I thought you didn't want us involved.'

'Some of us still *don't*. And, hey, if you don't want to . . .'

'No,' said Elsa. 'We do want to help. They put us in that prison, remember?'

'I figured as much. Still, anything too dangerous you leave to us.'

Elsa looked relieved. 'I'm fine with that.'

Elsa left the others and was on the way back to her bedroom when she heard a voice calling out. She halted in the middle of the corridor.

'Help!' The voice was coming from behind the nearest door and stirred her to move. She tried the handle. It was locked.

As she stepped away, she noticed that the skirting-board was coming away from the wall. She knelt down and tugged it. A small key clattered on to the floorboards.

Elsa studied the key, then put it in the lock. There was a click and she pushed the door open a fraction.

'Hello?' she said cautiously. 'Is there someone there?'
There was no answer.

She stepped inside, waiting for her eyes to unravel the mass of shapes in the darkness. Then something growled: a vicious animal sound.

Elsa shrieked and backed away.

'Please, please,' a voice whispered. 'I – I won't hurt you.'

Elsa froze. As her eyes adjusted, she saw a man lying in a bed against the far wall. *A prisoner*, was her first thought, noticing the buckles and straps across his body that rendered him immobile.

Her voice came out timidly. 'Who are you?'

'My name is Saul . . . Are you one of us, child?' His voice was weak and hoarse.

'Um, I don't know what you mean,' Elsa said, stepping closer, after giving the straps another look. The man – Saul – had long matted hair. He wore a white nightgown. His bulging eyes showed signs of a fever, or madness. Dried blood was flecked around his nose and lip.

'I have it too, little one,' the man said. He shut his eyes and began groaning.

'What's wrong? Are you OK?'

'The sickness,' he said, 'it's getting worse . . . every hour now . . . the nosebleeds . . . the blackouts . . . I don't know what's real any more . . .'

'I don't understand!' Elsa exclaimed. 'Please, just tell me what's wrong.'

'There's nothing they can do.'

Elsa's eyes darted over him anxiously, trying to work

out whether he was mad or mistaken. *Maybe he really is sick*.

'Soon it will happen to all of us. I'm just the first . . . It will claim every last one of us.' Saul looked up at her sadly. 'Breathe no word of this to the others, child . . . The Guild mustn't know you have spoken with me.'

'I promise,' Elsa said. 'I won't tell anyone. I just want to help you.'

'You can help me. All you have to do is to take the pillow from behind my head and put it down over my face . . . It is the only way . . . the only way to stop the sickness . . .'

'No!' Elsa hurried away from the bed, shaking her head.

Tears began streaming down Saul's face. 'Please, little girl. Please. If you don't, then you must let me go. So I can do it myself.'

Elsa began to cry too, loud forceful tears, each one jolting her.

'They'll keep me here forever, in a living hell . . . I've begged them, but they won't kill me,' he whispered. 'They keep me here so I won't harm myself. But it's too late; I am already harmed. There is no cure. None.'

Elsa brushed her tears away with her sleeve. 'I'm sorry,' she said. 'I'm sorry.'

With that, she ran out of the room, slammed the door shut behind her and locked it, wishing she had never let her curiosity get the better of her.

11

Luthan pushed the binoculars towards Julian. The pair were sitting in a maroon-coloured four-wheel drive, which was parked a street away from Stephen's office in the city's financial district.

'We need some idea of Nover's routine,' Luthan murmured. 'And his security.'

Julian peered through the binoculars and passed them back to Luthan. 'I've already told you, I know a quicker way to draw him out. This little spying act is a waste of time.'

'You want to stay with us, you do things properly. *Our way.* I wonder if your parents would be impressed with the way you speak to your elders, Julian.'

Julian looked away. 'My parents wouldn't care. They're dead.'

Luthan was silent. He watched the boy's downcast reflection in the window, sheathed in misty light. Julian put a pale hand to his brow.

'They're dead and I caused their death,' he muttered. 'You know what I was doing just before they died?

Playing with toy cars. Making them crash. The Ability –
my Ability – made it happen.'

'That doesn't mean you were responsible, Julian. It
could just be a –'

'A coincidence?' Julian snorted, turning to Luthan. 'I
thought that was the way this whole thing worked, by
causing strings of coincidences . . .' He trailed off, fiddling
anxiously with the plastic latch on the glove compartment.

'So that's why you've been reluctant to train with us.'

'I don't want it,' Julian replied, looking away. 'I don't
need it. I don't understand why we have it or where it
comes from. But it's a curse. You people only see the
good side of it.'

Julian grabbed the handle and pushed open the door.
I have to get out, he panicked, feeling suddenly
claustrophobic. He hurried past an enormous queue of
Stephen's admirers, who were waiting to accost him for
an autograph. It was bizarre to think that a businessman
could attract the kind of screaming crowd usually
reserved for pop stars; then again, Stephen was just
twenty-one and handsome.

'Julian!' Luthan called out. Julian glanced over his
shoulder and continued on his way.

What did he know anyway? What did any *of them
know?* They might have trained themselves to use the
Ability – whatever it was – but what remained clear to
Julian was that the blind were leading the blind.

'I'm scared I'm going to make a fool of myself,' Julian
heard one of Stephen's fans say.

'I know! I feel really light-headed,' another agreed.

Probably because your head's empty, Julian very nearly said and began to feel a little better about himself.

As he was crossing the road, a black limousine rounded the corner and parked. There was an almighty cheer from the crowd.

Julian looked round to see Luthan waving frantically from the car, but, before he could react, the door of the limousine opened and Stephen emerged from it, bowing theatrically and grinning and giggling to himself as four security personnel positioned themselves around him. As if by some sixth sense, Stephen turned in Julian's direction. Julian lowered his eyes but it was too late; he had been seen. He walked away quickly.

'Aww,' Stephen announced, 'one of my fans is leaving. I think he's a little too embarrassed to meet me!'

Julian ignored him and carried on walking.

'Now, that really hurts my feelings,' Stephen said, pouting.

The crowd all sighed collectively in sympathy. 'But *we* still love you, Stephen!' one of them screamed.

Stephen grinned. 'Yes, yes. I know you do. That's why whoever brings me that boy will win a ride with me in my helicopter!'

Julian stopped at the collective ear-splitting shriek from the group. The sound chilled him. He looked over his shoulder just in time to see the crowd rushing at him.

A girl threw herself at Julian's feet, laughing and screaming, 'I've got him! I've got him, Stephen!' Julian tripped over on to the icy pavement, his hands smarting at the impact. He tried to kick free, but then another girl grabbed his other foot and one leapt on to his back. Such was the chaos that even Stephen's burly security guards seemed unwilling to break it up. At the bottom of the pile Julian was winded, as more and more bodies piled on top of him until he could feel his ribs caving into his body and random hands pulling and plucking and scratching at him. A stray fingernail jabbed his eye, another his mouth.

He bit down as hard as he could. There was a squeal of pain in between the laughter and cheers and yells of 'I got him! I was first!' Eventually some of the girls began fighting one another, frenziedly declaring ownership of their prize.

'Get off!' he gasped, unable even to scream. 'Please . . . I . . . I can't breathe . . .'

At once there was a faint *whomp*. That familiar sound.

'Julian!' he heard a voice cry. 'Julian!'

Some of the weight lifted from his back. There was another *whomp*. *An ibis*. More of Stephen's fans climbed away, screaming.

Julian managed to knock some of the fans away and crawled to his feet, clutching his ribs. He knelt by a car, doubled over and gathering his precious breath. He saw Luthan firing an ibis to scatter the crowd.

As Julian was recovering, a polished designer shoe kicked him in the mouth. His head slammed back against the car. 'Imbecile!' Stephen shrieked. 'Worthless, useless little peasant . . . I know you hacked my website! Thought you'd come back and intimidate me, did you?'

He launched a second kick but Julian dodged the attack. Stephen's foot struck the car and he squealed, clutching his foot. Mustering some inner reserve of energy, Julian pounced and knocked him to the pavement. The two rolled around together, with Stephen screaming for his security guards. Suddenly Julian felt a jolt as Luthan grabbed him by the scruff of the neck.

'Get to the car,' Luthan snapped. A little dazed, Julian took a moment to locate it. Then he ran towards it and threw himself in the back. Luthan leapt inside and drove the car on to the pavement, avoiding the mass of teenage girls.

'Not going to thank me?' Julian mumbled out of a bleeding mouth, holding his side as the car weaved in and out of traffic.

'Thank you? You just started a riot with the wealthiest man in the country,' snarled a furious Luthan. 'What makes you think I'm going to thank you for anything, you little twerp?'

'This. This is why,' Julian wheezed, holding something between his forefingers and thumb. He presented Luthan with a wallet. He opened it, plucked out a swipe card and threw the wallet on to the seat. 'Access to his office. I'll bet his Pledge key is there.'

Luthan snatched the swipe card from Julian, looked at it for a moment, then at Julian, before shoving the card in his pocket.

'Good work, Julian,' he said resentfully.

12

Jes was in her bedroom, cramming clothes into a holdall when a flustered Elsa appeared.

'Jes, you're not gonna believe what just happened to me –'

'Nothing surprises me any more,' Jes mumbled, not looking up.

Elsa went to speak, but stopped. 'Why are you packing? Where are you going?'

Jes pummelled the clothes inside the holdall and zipped it shut. 'I'm leaving.'

'Leaving? Wait a minute, Jes – you can't just go. What'll you do?'

'I don't have the Ability, Elsa. I'm not one of *you*. I never will be.' Jes looked at Elsa sadly.

'But that doesn't mean –'

'It means there's no point in me being here any more. I'm going *home*. It's where I belong. It's the only place I belong.'

'But what if someone comes after you?'

'I can defend myself,' Jes snapped. 'I'm stronger than I look. I don't need some magic power to look after myself.'

She slung the bag over her shoulder and hurried along the corridor. When she reached the stairs, Ryan was making his way up.

'Jes?' he said. 'What's with the bag? Are you going somewh–'

'I am – yeah,' she muttered and stepped towards him. 'I'm going home. Thanks, Ryan,' she whispered. 'For everything.'

Jes leant in and kissed him on the lips. Then she panicked and pulled away from him. *God, what did I just do?* It was like something had taken control of her.

'I – I have to go,' she said, hurrying down the stairs.

Ryan called after her, but she ignored him.

It was late afternoon when Jes arrived in her home town to an overcast sky and pavements lined with slushy ice.

She'd taken a twenty-pound note from Anton's wallet to pay for her trains. She was sure he wouldn't mind – not that she could ask him. Regardless of whether or not she was one of *them*, the Guild didn't think she'd be safe on her own. Alyn used to think the same thing too; he didn't trust her.

Things don't look any different here, she thought as she left the station. Except everything felt somehow *smaller*, more insignificant. She wandered along the pavement, past a parade of shops. She walked through the town and cut through the suburban roads to her family home.

But when she arrived there she stopped and her mouth opened in silent protest.

Their six-bedroomed house was adorned with scaffolding, and the brickwork was charred and the lower windows boarded up. The front garden where she used to play as a little girl was blackened and spoiled, and her bedroom window was missing, exposing the dark cement. Everything that she had been desperate to return to was in ruins.

Jes backed away and bumped into a woman behind her.

'Jes?' said an old woman, peering at her.

'Mrs Rhodes,' said Jes. She looked back at the house, unable to find the words.

'Jes, your parents – they aren't here. They're staying somewhere else . . .'

'What happened?' Jes said. 'Are they OK?'

'They're fine.' The old woman touched Jes's arm. 'It was the hooligans who did this, during one of the riots. Yours wasn't the only house. They got another two at the end of the road . . .'

Jes felt her throat tighten.

'Jealousy,' the old woman went on. 'That's why they targeted this street. The whole country's falling apart. No one cares about each other any more. They're animals. They just want to destroy everything.' She touched Jes's arm. 'Your parents have been so worried about you. It damn near ruined them, you going off like that . . .'

'I need to find them,' Jes said, after a few moments staring at the devastated house. 'You have to help me.'

13

The cell was just big enough for Henry to manage twelve steps in a circle. How many circles had he trodden into the cement? A hundred? A thousand? He had lost count.

There was still no news. Maybe the Guild weren't coming. Maybe they'd given up. *I wouldn't blame them*, he thought. After all, the prison was impenetrable; there was little chance they could free everyone.

No, Luthan would never leave him here. He'd do anything to bring him back. The two had been together for a decade. They were best friends, brought together by love, and the Guild. Henry smiled as a memory flashed into his thoughts of when they had last spoken, just before he had left. Luthan had warned him not to go to the prison, at least not alone. But Henry was too independent. *Too stubborn*. He paused, hearing footsteps in the corridor outside, and pressed his ear to the door.

'I've come to see the prisoner,' he heard Susannah say.

'Any idea who he is yet?' the guard replied.

'He's just a crazy old man who's been living in the

forest. He was trying to free all of them. Best we keep him here until we speak with the authorities.'

'If you don't mind me saying, things have been getting weirder in this place by the minute,' the guard said. 'I don't know what the hell's going on any more.'

'No need to worry. This is a remote facility for young offenders surrounded by the . . . calming influence of nature.'

As she said this, there was a rumble of thunder.

'I think Michael in cell fourteen has some sort of lock pick. Would you mind checking it for me?'

The guard gave a distinctly dissatisfied nod and left.

'Just "a crazy old man who's been living in the forest",' Henry repeated as she entered his cell. 'Thanks for that.'

'More and more of the children are getting sick,' Susannah said. 'Having nosebleeds. Another girl has started having blackouts.'

'You have to stop making them watch the films,' Henry replied. 'Remove all of the subliminal messages. Stop making them manipulate reality. Stop everything! Otherwise they'll all lose their minds . . . It'll kill them!'

'But Stephen . . .'

'Stephen won't know. Stephen isn't here. You're in charge. It's down to you, Susannah. But you need to act soon. You need to act *now*.'

14

It had been several hours since Alyn had been taken back to the abandoned church. He sat on the floor in the aisle between the pews, staring at the flickering candle flame.

In his hands was the photograph of Luthan, the man he'd been ordered to bring to Emmanuel. If he obeyed, Luthan was as good as dead.

A door creaked suddenly and Alyn sat up, alert. Footsteps clicked over the stone, before halting.

'Something on your mind, Alyn?' Emmanuel said, walking slowly towards him.

'You have my father,' Alyn murmured, refusing to look at him. 'You threatened to kill him. And my friends.'

Emmanuel lifted the black scarf from his coat and folded it over one of the wooden pews. 'Let's hope it doesn't come to that. You understand what you have to do.'

'You want me to bring you Luthan.' Alyn shook his head. 'Even if I wanted to, I couldn't.'

'Such little faith in yourself. You have no idea what

you are capable of.' Emmanuel paused, looking up at the rafters. 'Do you see that bird?'

Alyn glanced up, but chose not to answer.

Emmanuel shut his eyes and waved his hand. Instantly a pigeon fell to the floor, unconscious.

'Visualize a sudden explosive flash in the centre of the creature's mind,' Emmanuel said. 'Now you try.'

Alyn looked up at the rafters. In response to the sudden collapse of its partner, a second pigeon was fluttering its wings anxiously.

Alyn closed his eyes. He imagined his locus, a butterfly, entering the mind of the pigeon to plunge it into sudden unconsciousness. But when he opened his eyes the bird had settled back on the beams with little concern.

'Again,' Emmanuel ordered. 'Your imagination is not strong enough.'

Alyn shut his eyes and tried again, tensing his jaw in concentration. Moments later, there was a flustered flapping of wings and the pigeon fell, landing a little way from the first.

'Good,' Emmanuel said, and picked up his scarf. 'Luthan has been following Stephen Nover as of late, but has been unable to get close. I'm meeting Nover tomorrow. I'm sure Luthan will be there. Bring him to me, Alyn.'

'Why can't *you* do it? I don't understand why it has to be me,' Alyn protested.

'Luthan is too adept. He'll be able to *sense* my

presence before I'm able to get close enough.' He began walking down the aisle, while Alyn sat motionless, staring at the unconscious pigeon. 'Prove your commitment to me, Alyn. Help me defeat the Guild.'

15

Jes arrived at a little house on the other side of town, clutching the address her neighbour had written on a piece of paper.

She rang the doorbell. Then she rang it again, and again, and kept jabbing the button until a shape appeared in the glass.

Jes's father threw open the door and stood looking at her for several seconds.

'Jes,' he said quietly.

Jes beamed at him, thumbing a tear away from the corner of her eye. 'Dad, I'm so pleased to see you,' she said.

He threw his arms round her and hugged her tightly and she cried and laughed.

'You promise me you're all right?' Jes's father said, after telephoning her mother to come home from work. 'And no one hurt you? Are you sure?'

Jes winced at the thought of the bullet wound in her side. *Tell my parents I was shot?* She decided it might be better to keep that a secret.

'I don't care what happened, Jes, I just want you to be honest with me . . .'

'No one hurt me, Dad,' she said. She took a deep breath to try and settle her nerves. 'I was in a prison. There were almost a hundred of us there, we –'

'A prison?'

'Yeah, but it wasn't a real prison. I mean, it looked like one and everything, but it wasn't *real* . . .'

'So a *fake* prison?'

Jes nodded. 'There was a reason for us being there, Dad.'

'I'd love to hear it . . .'

'You wouldn't believe me if I told you,' she mumbled.

'Try me.' He put his arm round her shoulder.

'The world's stranger than you think,' Jes answered. 'Than anyone thinks.' Her voice became distant and ethereal. 'There are people who have this power . . .'

'*Power?* What kind of power?'

'They can influence probability, chance, by manipulating coincidences. They can make things happen, Dad.'

'How do you know all of this?'

'Because I was one of them.'

'You . . . *were?*'

'I've lost the Ability, though. Somehow. The Pledge, this group of billionaires, kidnapped us and were using us to manipulate things for them. And people. They were trying to repair the country . . .'

Jes's father looked lost. Then slowly he began to laugh. 'Jes,' he said in between breaths, 'someone's made a fool out of you . . . They've been playing a joke on you or something . . .' He squeezed her arm. 'This is the craziest thing I've ever heard.'

'Imagine how I felt,' she said. 'Then we found the Guild and they –'

'*The Guild?*'

'They're a training order. For people with the Ability.'

Jes's father laughed again, throwing his head back.

'Dad, stop. Please.'

'We thought you were dead,' he whispered. 'We thought something terrible had happened. And it turns out you were in the plot of some science-fiction story. Or fantasy. Come to think of it, I don't even know what genre it is.'

Jes smiled. 'Me neither, Dad.'

Jes's father put his arms round her again. The pair sat in silence, while outside it started to rain.

16

Ryan threw another shot at the punchbag, then a second and a third. He wore a scruffy red jumper, borrowed from Anton, inside out, in defiance of the offending football team logo on the front.

'I'm knackered,' Ryan panted, wiping his forehead.

'*You* wanted some last-minute training before we go after Blythe,' said Anton. Then, as Ryan resumed, he added, 'Anyway, keep your other hand up. You're leaving yourself open.'

'Look, I *know* how to punch, all right?' Ryan grumbled.

'In the playground. But you come up against someone who knows what they're doing and you're stuffed.'

Ryan threw a few more punches quickly.

'Someone annoyed you?' Anton asked with a smile.

Ryan frowned and landed another shot on the bag. It was Jes's decision to leave. He'd been worrying about her for the past day, and with no way of contacting her he was anxious that they might never see each other again.

Ryan stopped punching the bag and leant over, gasping

for air. He mopped a film of sweat from his forehead. 'So we're basically gonna follow some rich drunk bloke and force him to give us a key. If we screw this up, we're gonna end up inside for real, you know.'

He waited until Anton had left and was about to resume his attack on the bag, but paused, taken by a memory of the night he was kidnapped. Even though it hadn't been that long ago, it seemed a lifetime had passed. Maybe it *was* another lifetime; after all, he was a different person now, wasn't he? Before then he'd spent his whole life with his mother on a rough estate in a free-fall of failing grades and petty crime, surrounded by people who'd already given up. What was the point in trying? There were times when it felt like he was suffocating under it all. Being dragged deeper into an inescapable pit.

Perhaps Nowhere was the best thing that could have happened to him – the first time he had actually ever been *free*. He straightened up, captivated by the swaying punchbag as if it were a pendulum. And some of the cold anger that had been carved into him over sixteen years finally began to thaw.

17

Luthan and Julian approached the skyscraper together, shielding their eyes from the low winter sun that was glinting off the surrounding glass buildings.

'This is your last chance, Julian,' said Luthan. 'Another stunt like last time and we're through. *You're* through.'

Julian smirked. 'Charming. Considering I'm the one who got you his swipe card. So, what's the plan?'

'The plan is you wait outside,' said Luthan.

'Where are you going?'

'To get Stephen's key, so we can put an end to everything.' Before he left, Luthan put a consoling hand on Julian's shoulder. 'It wasn't your fault, Julian.'

Julian looked away. 'I don't want to talk about it. I –'

Luthan held him. 'No running away, Julian. Just look at me. And listen. The Ability doesn't usually develop until eight or nine. You were too young to have caused your parents' accident. It wasn't your fault.'

Julian lifted his head, studying Luthan's eyes for their truth.

'Henry would tell you the same. And he discovered it after all, so he should know, shouldn't he?'

'You swear to me you're –'

'Telling the truth? Yes, Julian.' He patted the boy's shoulder. 'You didn't cause the accident that killed your parents.'

Julian watched him with some suspicion, which eventually eased. 'Thank you,' he said quietly. He gave a strained smile.

'Wait for me by the fountain. I'll be back soon.'

Julian watched him leave and put his hands in his pockets. A peculiar numb sensation washed over him.

It wasn't my fault.

18

Alyn had been waiting near Stephen's skyscraper all morning. He was starting to think Emmanuel might be mistaken about Luthan making an appearance, but a quarter of an hour later, the Guild's leader appeared, walking briskly towards the entrance to the skyscraper.

Alyn pulled a scarf across the lower half of his face and hurried after him. The wind was icy, roaring at his ears and making his eyes water.

He thought of his father tied up on the floor of Emmanuel's warehouse. Alyn had called him shortly after arriving in London and asked him for help. But what had he done? Nothing at all. He hadn't believed a word Alyn had said. And, even if he had believed it, chances are he wouldn't have cared. He'd been out of Alyn's life long enough.

Luthan went inside the skyscraper. Alyn waited a couple of minutes before following him through the revolving doors. A security guard looked up, but Alyn shut his eyes and gave a gesture with his hand. At that moment, two decorators hauling a large piece of panelling abruptly changed direction, blocking him from view. He hurried across the marble floor in pursuit of Luthan.

If Alyn did what Emmanuel asked of him, Luthan was as good as dead. But, if he disobeyed, there was a chance Alyn would never see his father alive again.

The lift opened and Alyn followed Luthan inside, merging with a crowd of office workers. He pulled his scarf across his face and leant against the handrail at the back. His palm was damp against the cold metal.

Luthan stepped out of the lift when it reached the top, followed by Alyn some moments later.

19

'So,' Stephen giggled, putting his feet up on the desk. 'I think we have lots to talk about, don't we?'

Emmanuel looked at the enormous portrait of Stephen on the wall and then back at Stephen.

'I understand you were Felix's adviser,' Stephen sneered. 'Presumably you advised him about this *Ability* . . . and it was you who made him have a heart attack. Like *that*!' Stephen said gleefully, clicking his fingers.

'He was threatening to expose us. I couldn't allow the project to be compromised.'

Stephen watched him carefully for a few moments. 'What exactly are *you* getting out of all of this?'

'I'm a philanthropist,' Emmanuel said. 'Just like the rest of you.'

Stephen looked unconvinced. 'My concern, Mr Emmanuel, or whatever your real name is, is what's stopping you doing the same to me?'

'If I wanted to harm you, I'd have already done so. Felix was a fool. His heart was no longer in it and I suspect that's why it gave out so . . . unexpectedly.'

'Ha!' Stephen shrieked. 'Yes!' He threw his head back, laughing.

'I've come here to discuss your plans, Stephen,' Emmanuel said to the hysterical young man sitting opposite him. 'To reaffirm my dedication to you, and to the rest of the Pledge.'

Stephen stopped laughing. 'What if you don't like my plans?'

Emmanuel watched him carefully. 'Then I might suggest an alternative. I am an adviser after all.'

Stephen released a thoughtful sigh and turned on his chair, looking out of the window at the city below.

'One idea I've been toying with is turning the children in the prison – the project – into a business,' Stephen pondered aloud. 'I'm sure the Vatican would pay for us to engineer a miracle or two on their behalf. Might convince a few more people to start believing in the old man in the sky, and it's not like they're short of the money, is it?'

Before Stephen could share the rest of his ideas, there was a knock on the door.

'Excuse me,' he said, and got up, stroking his silk tie. He walked over to the door and opened it.

'You,' he hissed, backing away. 'How did you get in here?'

'How do you think?' Luthan raised his hands. 'I'm not going to hurt you. I want to make you an offer.'

'What kind of offer?'

'An exchange. I give you one of the escaped inmates

in return for the prisoner you have in Nowhere. His name is Henry.'

Stephen narrowed his eyes, as if sensing Luthan's desperation. 'I have an important guest. Now leave before I have my security escort you out.'

'I have one of the children with me now.'

Stephen's eyes seemed to sparkle with excitement. 'Where?'

Luthan slumped with shame. He lowered his eyes.

'He's waiting outside by the fountain, wearing a green coat. But I must have your word, Stephen. You must promise to give me Henry.'

Alyn had caught the end of Luthan and Stephen's conversation from round the corridor and recoiled in disbelief.

One of his friends was in trouble; Luthan was a traitor to the Guild. He had to tell them.

He dashed into the lift. As soon as it reached the ground floor, he got out and sprinted past the reception, almost slipping on the marble.

He pushed his way through the revolving doors, nearly knocking the security guard off his feet and running through crowds of office workers.

'Alyn?'

Alyn turned. Julian was sitting on the stone fountain.

'Julian!' Alyn panted. 'Get out of here!'

Julian raised a contemptuous eyebrow. 'Hmm. Nice to see you too.'

As he said this, three large men in suits came rushing out of the revolving doors.

'There he is!' one of them shouted, pointing at Julian. 'The kid in the green coat.'

Alyn grabbed Julian and shoved him. 'None of you are safe! You have to run . . . I'll try to hold them off.'

Julian saw the approaching men and darted into the crowd. Alyn shut his eyes. Just seconds later, a pram slipped out of a woman's hands and rolled towards Julian's pursuers. The man at the front stopped, skidded on a patch of ice and landed on his back. The pair behind him struggled to keep their balance and tripped, collapsing in a pile on the ground.

By the time they got to their feet, Julian had gone. Alyn gave them a final look and hurried away through the crowds.

20

'I need the toilet,' Elsa said, pressing her face against the car window. She, Pyra, Charlie and Harlan had set off at noon in search of Antonia.

'Again?' Pyra said. 'We were only just at a service station . . .'

'I know. It's because I get nervous!'

'Can you wait?'

'Um.'

'Um *what*, Elsa?' said Pyra.

'I think so.'

'Think so? Not good enough. This is an expensive car . . .'

Elsa flopped against the seat and crossed her arms grumpily. 'Never have kids!'

'Never gonna.' Pyra looked at Elsa and allowed a brief smile to fall across her lips. She fiddled with the radio.

'. . . sightings of a missing boy, Harlan Jahari, who disappeared twelve months ago. The boy was reportedly seen in an amusement arcade in south London, where he was recognized and quickly fled . . .'

'You idiot,' Pyra growled to Harlan who was dozing on the back seat.

'Hmm? What did I do?'

'You were seen!' Elsa exclaimed. 'You'll end up bringing everyone to our doorstep!'

'Gambling too,' Pyra muttered. 'This is a breach of our code.'

Harlan crossed his arms. 'But it's not like I was wasting it. I was going to send the money I won to my parents –'

'How much have you been using the Ability?' asked Charlie.

Harlan shrugged. 'I don't know. Haven't been keeping count . . .'

Elsa pressed her head against the window, thinking of Saul, the man in the locked room. She desperately wanted to let her secret out, but remembered the promise she had made.

'Antonia's estate is over forty acres of land. We're gonna have to park up and hike the rest of the way.'

'Great,' Elsa grumbled. After her escape from the prison, another trek was the last thing she wanted to do.

Having left the car on a deserted road just off the motorway, the group checked a compass and set off into the woodland. Before too long, the sound of the streaming traffic disappeared altogether.

Elsa walked alongside Harlan, some way behind the others. 'Can I tell you something, Harlan?'

'Sure,' he said.

'I don't think you should keep using the Ability.'

Harlan snorted under his breath. 'You don't understand how important it is . . .'

'But it's not everything, right? I mean, you might be able to make a coin land on its edge or a bulb get a bit dim, if you think about it hard enough . . .' She paused. 'But *I* can cartwheel. I can do somersaults on trampolines and I can run faster than most boys in my year.' She shook her head at him and hurried to catch up with the others.

After walking for an hour the sky started to darken to winter-blue. A few solitary raindrops started to fall, looking almost silvery in the subdued light.

'We should camp here for the night,' Pyra said, once they were sheltered by trees. 'Then we'll head to Antonia's mansion first thing in the morning.' She took off her rucksack.

Elsa hadn't quite decided if the surrounding trees were intimidating or comforting. She watched Harlan and Charlie struggling to put up the tents.

'You coming to help me find some firewood, Elsa?' asked Pyra.

Elsa nodded. They went a little way from the campsite, Elsa skipping alongside Pyra. It was growing increasingly difficult to see much ahead of them.

'So what happens if we don't find these keys?'

'We will find them,' Pyra said. She leant over and

grabbed a branch, checking it with her fingertips for dampness. 'We'll find them and the project will be stopped. All of the other kids who are prisoners will be free.'

Elsa muttered something under her breath.

'What did you say?'

Elsa shook her head.

'You can tell me, Elsa. I don't bite. Not much anyway.'

'I was just –' Elsa paused – 'I was just wondering what happens next. What's gonna stop the Pledge from doing it again? What's gonna stop people like *us* being used?'

Pyra reached down for another branch but stopped. 'Luthan wants the Pledge wiped out,' she said.

'Wiped out?'

'Finished. Destroyed. *Dead*. Want me to keep going, or do you get the picture yet?'

Elsa shook her head again. 'What do *you* want?'

'I agree with him.'

Elsa grabbed her arm. 'We aren't *just* doing this to get the keys, are we? You're going to harm them, aren't you?'

'We're going to do whatever we have to do to keep us safe, kid.'

'But I thought we were supposed to be the good guys, Pyra! We'll be just as bad as they are! I did something, when we were on the streets. I tried stealing. I know what I did was wrong, but . . .' She looked distressed. 'In prison they told us we were bad people so we'd believe it but I never did, I promise. I just want to do what's right now, that's all.'

Pyra narrowed her eyes at Elsa. 'Doing what's right means destroying the Pledge.'

Elsa wanted to change Pyra's mind, but it was already made up; she had seen too much wrong in the world to ever see what was right with it. Elsa carried the wood back to camp with a bitter taste in her mouth.

21

Jes curled her hands round the mug of tea, as she sat in her parents' new home. The pair watched her, not saying a word.

Jes's mother finally spoke. 'I think we need to talk properly. No more games, no stories. We'll listen to you. To everything. And we won't judge you. We won't . . . we won't say anything. I promise.'

'But I've told you, Mum,' Jes said. 'I've told you everything.'

Her mother took her hand with a firm grip. 'Please, Jes.'

Jes pulled away. 'I've *told you* what happened to me.' She put her hand to her eyes. 'I did something terrible.' Her parents remained silent. 'I hurt someone . . . one of the guards . . . He was sick . . . cruel . . . I was just so frustrated and angry. I didn't mean to do it . . . I was just so angry . . . I still am . . .'

She hoped one of her parents might say something to break the silence.

Eventually it was her father who spoke. 'Jes, we know

you've – how can I say this? – *changed* a little in the past year or so.'

Jes looked up at him. 'I don't understand what you mean.'

'We found alcohol in your bedroom,' he said.

'Several bottles,' her mother added.

Jes was taken aback. 'Me and the girls had a drink one night when they came over ages ago . . . That's not got anything to do with what happened to me.' The frustration was beginning to swell in her throat. 'If you're trying to say I've gone off the rails or something, you're wrong . . . What happened to me was real!'

Her mother got up and perched on the side of Jes's chair, putting an arm round her shoulder. 'I think something terrible has happened to you . . . and you're trying to block it out . . . The mind does this, it makes stories out of things . . . and this is your way of dealing with it. I think it'd be a good idea if you got some help.'

Shaking her head, Jes got to her feet and ran upstairs to the bathroom. She retched into the toilet. Her face was hot, her head pounding. She wiped the hair from her face and pressed her brow against the porcelain tiles. Downstairs, her parents were talking. Jes crept on to the landing.

'I think we should call them,' she heard her father say. 'Otherwise there's a good chance she's just going to run away again.'

Call who? Jes strained her ears and listened as her

father picked up the phone and spoke quietly into the handset.

'Jes?' her mother called from below. 'What are you doing?'

Jes ran into the nearest bedroom and slammed the door behind her. Piled around the room were boxes of her old belongings. Her eyes wandered over a couple of plastic bags, bursting with books, when she spotted the long neck of her stuffed giraffe. She'd had it since she was a baby.

She walked over, pulled the giraffe out of the bag and held it against her chest. Her throat tightened.

I should never have come back, she thought, panicking as she sat with her back against the door. *I should've stayed with the others.* Out of everything she had thought might happen to her, her parents not believing her was the last.

It wasn't much later that Jes heard the sound of a car pulling up outside. She stood and crept over to the window. Two people got out: a man wearing a suit, with an identity badge attached to a blue lanyard, and a woman, who was speaking into a phone.

Jes watched out of the window as her mother opened the door and quickly brought the strangers inside.

'Jes?' said a man's voice on the stairs. 'I'm Doctor Burroughs. My colleague and I are here to speak with you . . .'

They want to take me away. They think I'm mad. Two pairs of footsteps travelled slowly up the stairs in time with each other.

Jes dragged a small table in front of the door. Then she ran to the window and levered it open. Cold air blew in.

'Jes,' the voice said. 'We're not going to hurt you. We just want to have a chat with you, if that's OK?'

There was a tap at her door and the handle turned.

'Can you please open it, Jes?' said a woman's voice.

Jes grabbed a coat from the nearest box. She scrambled on to her desk and slipped outside the window. She looked down at the hedge below that she hoped would break her fall and jumped.

The fall sent a jolt through her legs and for a few moments she felt like she might not be able to get back up. Her arms were covered in thin cuts and scratches from the misshapen hedge.

As soon as she could stand, she staggered to her feet and ran.

22

It took Alyn a few hours to find the warehouse. He paused behind a van, scanning the yard for any of Emmanuel's men who might be keeping watch. There were none around, but the shutter was half-raised. That meant they probably weren't going to be gone for long. He crept nearer and rolled underneath.

The warehouse was submerged in darkness. Alyn crept inside, zigzagging behind a row of crates. He paused by one, thinking he'd heard a sound from above.

He lowered himself down, peering round the wooden slats, scanning for movement. There was no one there. Alyn sped up the metal staircase on to the walkway. He held his breath as the stairs echoed. Once he was there, he darted along on tiptoes and came to the little room where his father had been held. He squinted through the glass window and saw his father lying on the floor.

His father looked up and groaned behind his gag. Alyn put his finger to his lips, then pushed the door open and ran inside.

'Dad, you OK?' he whispered. He pulled down his father's gag and began untying the rope round his hands.

'It's you!' he gasped. 'My boy. My boy. Why'd you come back for me?'

Alyn loosened one of the knots. 'I wasn't going to leave you.'

His father snorted. 'Like I left you all those years ago. You're a better man than I am, son.'

Alyn unfastened the last knot. 'I know I am,' he said coolly.

This was enough to silence his father. He put his hand across his face.

'Stop feeling sorry for yourself.' Alyn threw the ropes aside and hoisted him to his feet. 'You need to get out of here.' Alyn steered him out of the room to the walkway. 'Don't go home. Don't go anywhere where they might find you. You're going to need to hide.'

'What about you . . .?'

Alyn stopped on the stairs. 'I don't know, Dad. I don't know what I'm going to do.'

They walked in silence back across the warehouse floor, checking for any of Emmanuel's followers. 'Thank you, boy,' Alyn's father murmured, once they reached the entrance. 'And I'm sorry.'

'Just go,' Alyn said.

His father then stopped and tapped the side of his nose. 'You're bleeding.' He gave his son a parting nod of what Alyn guessed to be respect, then crawled underneath the shutters and ran.

Alyn checked his nose. There was a red smear of blood across his fingertips.

He walked back through the warehouse, pinching his nose with his head tilted back. It was only then that he noticed a dry, powdery scent lingering beneath the aroma of blood.

He lifted the tarpaulin from the nearest crate and took a sharp intake of breath. *Explosives.*

Alyn tore back the covering on another crate and then another, until it became alarmingly clear that all the crates were packed with enough explosives to devastate an entire area of the city.

A familiar voice spoke from outside: 'I need a helicopter to take me to Scotland. Have it here within the hour.'

Before Alyn could find somewhere to hide, Emmanuel lifted the shutters and paused upon seeing the figure before him.

'I'm disappointed, Alyn,' Emmanuel eventually said. 'I gave you such an opportunity –'

'An opportunity?' Alyn could feel his heartbeat in his throat. 'You didn't give me any choice.'

'There's always a choice, Alyn.' Emmanuel stepped closer. Alyn went to push past him, but was grabbed. Emmanuel's grip was icy, and his fingers pushed deep into Alyn's throat.

'I've planned this for so long,' Emmanuel hissed. 'No one is going to stand in my way. Not you, not the Guild . . .'

Emmanuel released Alyn, launching him against the shutters, where Alyn fell to the floor. At that moment, the door on the far side of the warehouse opened and several members of Emmanuel's gang appeared. Alyn scrambled under the shutter as fast as he could and ran.

23

When Elsa opened her eyes a dull blue light was pouring through the thin fabric of her tent. It took her a moment to remember where she was. *We're going to find Antonia. To find her Pledge key*, she announced to herself. This gave her the motivation to sit up.

As Elsa was rubbing her eyes, Pyra unzipped the tent flap.

'Get yourself together, kid,' she said. 'We're leaving soon.'

Elsa stumbled out. The fire they had made last night was a mass of black ash among the curled dead leaves on the wet soil. Crusts of snow and ice were dotted across the grass. Elsa walked over to a sleepy-looking Harlan, who was zipping up his rucksack.

'Here,' he said, handing her his ibis. 'Take it. Just in case.'

'Didn't know you still had it! You sure?'

Harlan nodded, rubbing the side of his head.

Elsa took the weapon and grinned. She instantly felt safer with it in her possession.

'Now, what about breakfast?'

'No time,' Pyra said. 'But if we get that key from Antonia you can have as much pizza and ice cream as you can eat. All right?'

Elsa looked down at her rumbling stomach and sighed. *Could I last another few hours?* she wondered.

When the tents were collapsed and packed away, the group set off in search of Antonia's mansion through the remaining woodland.

Charlie was following a compass alongside Harlan while Elsa trailed Pyra at the back.

'Keep up,' Pyra said.

Elsa huffed, struggling to keep her backpack secure. 'If she gives us this key, you promise you won't hurt her?'

Pyra shrugged, hoisting her own rucksack further up her back. 'I'm not promising anything.'

Elsa looked at her sadly. 'There are good people in the world. I just think you've had some bad experiences . . .'

Pyra stopped walking and glared at Elsa. 'Since when did I ask for counselling from some damned thirteen-year-old?'

Harlan glanced over his shoulder at the pair. He seemed weary. 'You two all right?'

'Fine,' Pyra said. 'Though you don't look so good, Harlan.'

'I – I feel a bit weird,' he said, and dropped to his knees without warning.

Pyra let go of her rucksack and ran over to Harlan.

'Harlan,' she said, slapping the side of his face.

'I – I can't concentrate . . .'

'How much have you been using the Ability, Harlan?' asked Pyra.

Drifting in and out of consciousness, Harlan struggled to talk. A stream of blood trickled out of his nose.

Elsa ran over and knelt down beside him. She grabbed Pyra's arm. 'Look,' she said. 'His nose . . .'

'I see it,' Charlie said. He dug in his pockets for a tissue. When he found one, he began mopping up the blood.

'What's going on?' Elsa cried. 'Can somebody just tell me?'

'You're going to need to stay with him, Charlie. Set up a tent with him in the woods back there, all right?'

Charlie nodded and knelt behind Harlan, lifting his head on to his lap. 'He's sick,' he said. 'He –'

He's got the same thing as Saul, Elsa thought, remembering the nosebleed. *The sickness.*

'Please be OK,' she begged. 'Don't go mad, Harlan.'

Pyra grabbed Elsa by the scruff of the neck and lifted her away. 'There's nothing we can do. Come on. Let's get going.'

24

Back in London, Jes sat on a bench near the station and put her head in her hands. '*Mad!*' She spat the word aloud in disbelief. 'They think I'm mad!'

The woman sitting beside her gave her a quick look and shuffled to the side.

'Oh, so *you* think I'm crazy too?' Jes said, glaring at her. 'Well, I'm *not*. There's nothing wrong with me.'

'No, I didn't mean anything, I just –'

Jes narrowed her eyes. 'If you had any idea what's happened to me ... But you don't! You don't have a clue what's going on, about the people who run this country ... about the kind of stuff they've been doing!'

The woman smiled politely and stood, gathering her bags.

'Wait!' Jes called back. 'I didn't mean that, I swear there's nothing wrong with me ...'

Jes's head sank back into her hands. She was cold and wet, and the scar on her side was aching. She stood slowly, and miserably trudged away into the crowds of pedestrians. There was only one place left for her to go, and that was back to the Guild.

After escaping Emmanuel, Alyn kept running until he was doubled over and huffing hoarse breaths of chilled air. His body ached and his legs felt close to buckling.

Alyn looked at his surroundings, a quiet suburban road, with little idea of where he was.

I have to find the others. I have to find Jes. He closed his eyes and imagined a butterfly moving quickly through the city and locating her, and drawing them both together. He felt the familiar tingling sensation in the back of his mind and then a sudden surge of light-headedness. Just moments later, he noticed a flattened cardboard box in the road, with THIS WAY UP printed on it beside an arrow. The 'up' was partially obscured with mud. *As good a start as any*, Alyn thought and hurried in the direction that the arrow pointed.

Alyn followed a multitude of signs that seemed to appear to him over the next hour or so. He travelled on trains and buses, causing the machines to stutter and ticket gates to falter. He felt like both a trespasser in the city and its possessor, able to move freely, wherever he wished.

Back in the prison, Jes had been the only one who'd kept him going. He had seen her briefly in the ballroom with the others. And in all the chaos she had disappeared.

Before then, he'd thought she was dead. Felix had told him that. When he had caught sight of her that night, Alyn had thought he was looking at a ghost. If only he knew where she was now . . .

When he eventually reached Tottenham Court Road, Alyn lowered himself against a shuttered shop window. Was this even working? It was almost midnight and there was no sign of Jes anywhere.

He shut his eyes and took a deep breath. The cold air sliced his throat. *Go left*, some voice within him urged.

Jes wiped the tears of frustration from her eyes. *Another dead end.* She had been walking in circles, spiralling deeper and deeper into a maze of unrecognizable roads.

'I'm looking for a block of flats called Hermes House,' she said, stopping a female pedestrian. 'It's in a pretty rundown area, there's a park just by it . . . and some shops . . .'

'I've never heard of it,' said the woman, giving her a sympathetic look and walking on.

As Jes turned back round, she collided with a man and tripped, landing on her hands.

'Oh, I'm so sorry,' he said, helping her to her feet.

'It's fine,' she said, and hurried across the road before the lights could change.

For the rest of Jes's journey, it seemed like the world was conspiring against her, nudging her towards certain directions. Her initial path was blocked by an ambulance after a man had collapsed; she unwittingly followed a flashing neon sign, which resembled an arrow but on closer inspection was simply broken.

If I had the Ability things would be easier, she thought. *If only I had someone with me, like Ryan, or ... or Alyn.*

Why had he been with James Felix, the leader of the Pledge? Had they really managed to *turn* him too?

When she reached the end of the road, Jes realized she was panting. The wound in her side ached with a dull soreness, made worse by the cold. She had no idea where she was.

'Jes?'

She looked up. There was a figure standing by a tree. It couldn't be ... She looked harder. 'Alyn?'

Alyn jogged towards her. His mouth was open and he was trying to speak, but the words caught on his lips.

'It worked,' he whispered, and started laughing to himself. 'It worked, Jes, it worked! I'm so happy to see you ...'

She looked at him with disbelief and growing suspicion. 'What worked?'

'Finding you,' Alyn replied. 'After everything I've seen ... after everything I've done ... this is the best of all.' He laughed again and stepped towards her.

Jes backed away and held out her hand for him to stop. 'Don't!'

'What?' Alyn showed her his hands. 'Jes, it's me. Alyn ...'

'I know everything,' she whispered. 'I know you're with *them*.'

Alyn looked confused. 'With who?'

'The Pledge.' Jes took another step back. 'Whose side are you on?'

'Yours,' Alyn answered. 'I've only ever been on your side.'

Jes looked at him for a few moments and her lip trembled. For some reason she believed him.

She hurried towards him and threw her arms round him. Warm tears fell across her face. She tried to speak but her words dissolved into sobs so she said nothing and hugged him in silence.

'I didn't think I'd ever see you again,' Alyn said. The pair were sitting together in a park a short way from where they'd met, holding hands. 'Then when I saw you guys at the opera house, I just . . .'

'They wouldn't let me near you,' Jes whispered. 'Elsa had been spying. She saw you with Felix and Blythe.'

Alyn smiled and shook his head. 'You can't have thought I'd ever join them, Jes?'

'What was I supposed to think? People have been turned before.'

Alyn let out a breath. 'I was trying to figure out what was going on. Felix – Felix was the leader, but he was the best of a bad bunch. Stephen is completely insane.'

'Yeah, we know all about him. We know he's a problem.'

Alyn turned to her. 'And he's not your biggest problem. There's someone else, even worse than Stephen. Emmanuel. The Pledge thinks he's an adviser . . .'

'But?'

'But he's planning on screwing everyone over. He wants the Pledge destroyed, the Guild destroyed. He's been organizing an uprising. A revolution. There'll be a blackout, no power for days, so he can take control of the city and –' Alyn searched for the word – 'and *rebuild* it. He wants politicians murdered, the banks destroyed. It'll be anarchy.'

'Seriously?'

Alyn nodded. 'He's been organizing this for years, Jes. He's unified all these different groups. There's an entire network of them. They have bombs, everything. As soon as the blackouts hit, all of this anger and everything that's been building up is just gonna explode. He also –' Alyn paused – 'he also has the Ability too. And he's more powerful than any of us.'

Jes looked at Alyn. 'We have to tell the Guild as soon as possible.'

'That's another problem,' Alyn said. 'Luthan. He was going to give Julian to Stephen.'

Jes gave him a look of disbelief. 'I know Julian's annoying, but Luthan wouldn't do that . . .'

'It's true, Jes. I was there. We need to tell the others – Elsa, Harlan, Julian . . . Ryan. None of you are safe while he's around . . .'

Jes pressed a hand against his face. 'I'm so glad you're back.' She kissed him lightly on the cheek. 'Let's go.'

25

Ryan tossed and turned on his thin mattress in the Guild's building. He and Anton had been following Blythe around the city, hoping for a moment when he might be unguarded. So far they had been unsuccessful.

A siren wailed in the distance. He could hear a group laughing somewhere in the park opposite. He turned again and the sheet tangled round his leg like a vine.

Eventually he stumbled out of bed, hitching up his scruffy tracksuit bottoms, and sat on the couch in his room. Through the wall he could hear Anton snoring loudly.

After a few minutes Ryan picked up the phone. He dialled a number, pausing before the last digit. His finger hovered over the button. He jabbed it aggressively and pressed Call.

The phone rang. It was the third time Ryan had called since he had been with the Guild. Each time had been in the dead of night, when he knew his mum probably wouldn't answer.

But this time she did. 'Hello,' she said in a voice so

tired and despairing that it seemed to peter out before it even reached his ear.

Ryan couldn't speak.

'Hello,' said the voice again, more irritated this time.

'Mum,' Ryan said.

Silence.

'Hello?' said his mother. 'Who's this? Who are you?'

'Mum, it's me,' Ryan said. 'It's Ryan.' As he said his own name, a lump stuck in his throat. He swallowed it.

'My son's missing,' said his mother.

'I'm not missing, Mum. I was kidnapped!'

'Kidnapped?'

'I swear it. Remember Dave and Callum and Carl, me best mates? It's me, Mum, honest.'

'Ryan,' she said quietly. 'What are you doing? What have you gotten caught up in?'

He laughed suddenly. How good it was to hear her voice again.

There was an intake of breath from the other end of the line.

'I've got to do something important,' Ryan said, 'and then I'll be home. I'll be coming home, Mum. As soon as this is done, all right? I'll be on the first train home.'

'"Something important",' his mother repeated, and started laughing but it was choked by tears. 'Whenever did you ever do anything bloody important apart from causing trouble with your mates? "Something important" . . .'

'I'm gonna help save the country,' he blurted out. 'That's what I'm gonna do.'

'"Save the country"?' His mother's voice became nasal, punctuated with tears. 'If you really are my son, come home in one piece,' she said, her voice softening. 'Just come home, Ryan. And don't go being a hero, all right? *Come home.*'

The call ended. Ryan held the phone in his hands until he could bear to hold it no longer and tossed it on to the chair.

26

A light fog was swirling by the time Pyra and Elsa arrived at the heart of Antonia's estate. Elsa had not been able to take her mind off Harlan, Saul and the sickness. *Was it contagious?* She kept checking her nose to make sure she wasn't bleeding.

In the distance loomed the spires and turrets of Antonia's mansion, shrouded in fog. Pyra walked towards the maze. Elsa grabbed hold of Pyra's arm, the ibis tight in her other hand.

'There must be an easier way in,' Elsa said, stepping in after her.

'Yeah, straight past her security. Why do you think she has this set up? She's a crazy old recluse . . .'

The scent of mud and damp dew filled the air. Elsa sniffed as she followed Pyra deeper into the maze.

'First dead end,' Pyra said. 'Come on, let's go back.' Tendrils of fog crawled between them like fingers.

'Can't see us getting any closer to that stupid house,' Elsa grumbled, squinting at the silhouetted mansion.

They walked down another couple of passages and came to another dead end.

'All right, I'm sick of this crap already,' Pyra said, and knelt down. 'Climb on.'

Elsa sat on Pyra's shoulders as Pyra carefully got to her feet. 'Can you see where we need to be?'

Elsa squinted through the fog. 'Um, I think so.' She peered forward, cupping her eyes. 'We need to be in the next row . . . I think it'll lead straight to the house!'

Pyra crouched down and Elsa hopped on to the grass. 'Trouble is, we've got to go all the way back over there.'

'You sure?'

'Um. Well, I don't know, but –' Elsa stopped and looked down at the bottom of the hedge. There was a patch of leaves missing.

'Maybe I could crawl under,' she offered, and immediately regretted opening her big mouth.

'Good thinking,' Pyra agreed, shoving her towards it. 'If you get freaked out, just come straight back to me, OK? I'll put my hand up.'

'Mm-hm,' Elsa said, already racking her brains for an excuse to get back to her as soon as possible.

She reluctantly crawled under the hedge and wriggled through the gap in the branches.

'Over here!' Pyra called from over the hedge, waving her hand.

Elsa nodded, scrambled to her feet and ran as quickly as possible through the fog and darkness. Her heart felt as though it was rattling inside her chest.

She turned left, then right, then ran on. Dead end. She ran back, then right again. But that seemed to be leading her further away.

'Hey!' Elsa shouted, looking for Pyra's hand. 'I can't see you!'

Her breath returned when she saw a pale hand, waving to her above the hedge. Shaken, Elsa turned and tripped. The ibis fell from her hand and was lost among the undergrowth.

'I've dropped the ibis!' she yelled. 'I can't see it! I've lost it!'

'Just stay put,' came Pyra's faint answer. 'Don't panic.'

Without the ibis, Elsa was vulnerable to whatever lurked in the maze. Before she could reason with herself, she ran and soon she became completely lost in Antonia Black's garden labyrinth.

'Elsa!' Pyra yelled. 'What's going on? What are you doing?'

Elsa ran left and right, flailing and stumbling. Panic was setting in; she felt it rising in her chest. Her breath quickened until it was hoarse and shallow.

'Pyra!' Elsa called out, but her voice had no strength. 'Pyra, where are you?'

She turned the next corner and became aware of something moving ahead of her. *What is that?*

'Pyra . . . there's . . . there's something here . . .'

She backed away, bumping against the hedge. The shape came at her through the fog. It was low, prowling, and only when it opened its jaws did Elsa realize what it was.

The dog leapt at her, easily knocking her on to her back. Then a second dog appeared, grabbing her skinny wrist in its jaws. Elsa wriggled, trying to free herself from the grasp of the creature. Then a third beast, larger than the rest, pounced at her and lowered its glistening white teeth to her throat.

'Stop!' said a female voice. The dogs paused obediently.

A woman moved towards the dogs. She was short, barely taller than Elsa, and was wearing a silk dressing-gown and an enormous fur coat.

'A child!' she exclaimed. 'A child, out here all alone, in my beautiful maze.'

Elsa, still struggling with her breath, could not speak.

'My name is Antonia Black,' the woman said. 'You and I obviously need to talk.'

27

When Jes and Alyn eventually found the Guild's headquarters it was just after six in the morning. Although still dark, traffic was slowly beginning to pour along the road.

Alyn kept looking at her to check that she was really there and not some phantom conjured by his desperate imagination.

She smiled. 'Why do you keep looking at me like that?'

'No reason. No reason at all.'

Alyn peered up warily at the grimy-looking block of flats.

Jes tapped in a code on the wall by the main entrance. There was a buzz and the gate was unlocked.

The pair went inside and up the lift. When it arrived at the top floor, they stepped out. Alyn looked around, astonished at the expansive palatial interior.

'Back already, Jes,' said Luthan, who emerged behind them. 'I hope you weren't followed.'

Jes smiled, a little embarrassed. 'This is Alyn. He's one of us.'

'Ah.' Luthan walked over and extended his hand. 'Alyn. Yes. I've heard lots about you. My name is Luthan.'

Alyn glared at him. 'I know who you are.' *And I know what you are.*

Luthan smiled. 'My reputation precedes me.'

'Where are the others?' Alyn said. 'Harlan and Elsa and . . .'

'Me?' Julian appeared, looking Alyn up and down. 'You'll be pleased to know I'm still here. The others are busy searching for the Pledge keys.'

'Pledge keys?' Alyn looked puzzled.

'It's a way of shutting down the prison,' Jes explained. 'Each of the Pledge has one. We think that together they trigger some kind of remote device . . .'

'That destroys the prison,' Julian clarified. 'It's the only way to end the project. Yes, very dramatic, I know.' He folded his arms. 'But there's a bit of a hitch – we haven't got any of them yet. For all we know, they don't even exist . . .'

'I *know* they exist. Because I have one,' Alyn said, and felt in his pocket for Felix's key. He felt a sharp stab of panic as his fingers found nothing but the soft lining of his coat.

'What's wrong?'

'It's not there . . . I must've dropped it in the warehouse. I'll have to go back and find it before Emmanuel does . . .'

Jes grabbed his arm. 'Not now,' she said. 'Stay here, rest. You look exhausted. You'll be no good to anyone.'

'Was it you who brought down that chandelier in the opera house, Alyn?' Luthan asked, stepping towards him.

Alyn's lack of response was as good an answer as any.

Julian rolled his eyes. 'Hate to be the sceptical one here, but I find that a little hard to believe. I mean, this Ability thing is about giving chance a gentle nudge. Making a chandelier fall from a ceiling is more like shoving chance off a cliff. Right, Luthan?'

'We don't know the limits of the Ability,' Luthan answered. He put his hand on Alyn's shoulder. 'Alyn, we're going to need you here, with us. But Jes is right. You need to rest. We still need Stephen's key. As soon as you've rested, the four of us can go after him.'

So you can try to exchange us, Alyn thought. He watched Luthan suspiciously.

'Please, Alyn,' Luthan insisted. 'Let's do it. Together.'

Alyn eventually nodded. 'Stephen it is. As long as you're with us, Luthan.'

Luthan smiled. 'Gladly.' He patted Alyn's arm. 'I'll see that a room is made up for you at once.'

28

Claude Rayner opened the door to Susannah's office. He was a tall, broad man with short grey hair and a penetrating stare that always seemed to be searching for the worst in someone.

Susannah was sitting behind her desk with several reels of film and a cutting knife, splicing in the subliminal messages that unconsciously harnessed the children's Ability.

'I'd prefer it if you knocked,' she said, nicking herself with the knife. A trickle of blood appeared on her finger.

Rayner studied her and walked over to the reels of film. 'These are going down to the projector room,' he said.

'Not yet,' Susannah answered. 'I'm not finished with them.'

Rayner nodded.

'Is there a reason you're here?'

Rayner snatched the nearest reel of film. He picked it up and held it towards the light.

'Claude,' she said, 'what are you doing? Give me that –'

She tried to grab the reel from his hands, but Rayner moved it away.

'This picture,' he said, 'it shows Nover behind bars. What are you trying to do? Use their power to get him arrested?'

Susannah got up and pulled him to the side. 'Look,' she whispered, 'Stephen has lost his mind. He wants to wipe out a third of the population. He's a lunatic!'

Rayner nodded. 'But a very wealthy lunatic. I can't let you mess this up.'

Susannah backed away. 'He's been paying you to check up on me, hasn't he?'

'I'm in the best place I've ever been in my life,' said Rayner. 'I've got everything I ever wanted. I'm not going anywhere.'

'That's what I thought too,' Susannah said. 'But you're wrong. Trust me, if you carry on, you'll want to get out, but they won't let you. I swear it. You think just the kids are prisoners, but they aren't – we *all* are.'

She glanced at the open door and pushed past Rayner, but he grasped her by the arm.

'Claude, let me go,' she protested, trying to wriggle free, and noticed a pyramid-shaped paperweight on her desk.

'Do what Nover wants,' Rayner growled. 'Or *I'll* do it. After all, how hard can it be to stick a few frames in a piece of film . . . ?'

Before he could say another word, Susannah grabbed the paperweight from her desk and slammed it into the side of his head.

Rayner staggered and fell against the wall. She turned, snatched the reels from the table, unravelled them, then launched them outside the window into the snow. She cast a final look at the unconscious guard, snatched her coat and ran out of the room.

Susannah bolted from the prison, pulling her coat tight round her. Her boots sank slowly into the sludge, squelching as she strode across the mounds of mushy snow.

Free from the spell of the place, it was starting to dawn on her what she had done: brainwashing, psychologically tormenting the children, forcing them to harm each other as punishment, conditioning them through pain into a web of lies that they had little choice other than to believe.

She had to get away before Rayner regained consciousness. There was a road, two miles from here. Once she was there she could flag down a vehicle and get a ride into the nearest town. *But then what?* The Pledge would come looking for her. She would have to flee the country.

As Susannah entered a clearing, she noticed a figure a short way up ahead. He wore a long overcoat and his eyes seemed almost black against the endless snow.

'You must be *the teacher*,' the man remarked, watching her.

'Who are you?'

'My name's Emmanuel,' he answered. 'I was an acquaintance of Felix's.'

'I don't have time to talk,' Susannah said, still making her way towards him. She looked over her shoulder. Far behind, in the trees, were the sounds of Rayner's voice and his ibis firing aimlessly into the snow.

'You won't make it out before he catches you,' Emmanuel said.

Susannah pushed on through the snow. She looked back at her trail of footprints. They would lead Rayner directly to her.

'Do something for me,' Emmanuel said. 'And I will help you.'

'Do *what* for you?'

Emmanuel removed an envelope from his pocket. 'Subliminal images. I want them inserted into the film.'

Panting, Susannah stopped. 'Who *are* you?' she said. An ibis fired again behind her. She flinched and glanced over her shoulder. She could just see Rayner's shadow moving through the trees. Susannah turned back to Emmanuel.

'If you listen to me, you won't ever have to worry about Stephen.' He watched her carefully, not blinking once.

'How do I know I can trust you?'

'Because I want him gone as much as you do. And if you do as I say,' Emmanuel said, proffering the envelope to her, 'the contents of this envelope will ensure it. Do we have a deal?'

Susannah looked up, just as a breathless Rayner emerged from the trees.

'I've told you, you're not going to mess this up,' the guard snarled, marching towards her, propelled by fury.

'Deal,' Susannah answered just as Rayner pointed the ibis at her.

Emmanuel turned to face Rayner and closed his eyes. Rayner squeezed the trigger, but the weapon refused to fire.

'She's under my protection now,' Emmanuel said, walking towards him. 'You can leave.'

It was the first time Rayner even acknowledged Emmanuel's presence. He threw down the useless ibis and marched towards them.

Emmanuel waved his hand and Rayner lost his balance on a patch of ice. He tried to steady himself but his legs shot out from underneath him and he landed on his back.

'You're one of *them*,' Rayner growled, raising himself up on a planted hand.

Before he could say another word, Emmanuel knelt behind him and wrapped his arms round Rayner's neck. There was a loud *crack* that echoed in Susannah's ears for what seemed like an eternity.

Emmanuel stood and handed her the envelope, which Susannah reluctantly took. She opened the envelope and flicked through the images.

'You want to cause a series of blackouts in the city. This will lead to chaos.' She looked up at him. 'But that's what you want, isn't it? Are you ... are you going to seize power?'

Emmanuel shook his head. 'No. I'm going to redistribute it. The prisoners must see these throughout the day and night. Set them in shifts, half the inmates at a time. Start at once.' He stepped menacingly towards her. 'Do *not* let me down.'

'Wait!' Susannah called, as Emmanuel walked away.

Soon he had disappeared completely. She looked at the envelope in her hand and then back in the direction of the prison.

29

Elsa was sat on a chair in the hall of Antonia's mansion. Antonia, flanked by her three ferocious-looking dogs, watched her intently. Elsa's eyes flickered around the room, gazing at the array of porcelain and marble statues and busts. A grandfather clock, probably centuries old, stood opposite, as though guarding her. Through the enormous curved windows, the fog had lifted and snow was falling again.

'So,' Antonia said. 'Tell me what you were doing on my estate.'

'I got lost,' Elsa said.

'You got *lost*. Hmm.' Antonia vacantly stroked the ears of one of the dogs. Its long pink tongue was dangling out of its open mouth. A web of drool sparkled on its teeth.

'Yup. Can I go now please?' Elsa went to stand but was pinned to the spot by the threat of the nearest dog, which began growling at her.

'What's your name, girl?'

'It's – it's Lydia.'

Antonia's eyes narrowed. 'I don't believe you. My dogs don't believe you. They can smell a liar. They –' she paused, watching as the dog moved stealthily towards a petrified Elsa – 'they enjoy the *taste* of a liar.'

'Elsa!' she squealed. 'That's my name.'

'A pretty name. Why are you here?'

Elsa was unable to take her eyes from the dog as it continued towards her. It snarled, baring a mouthful of teeth.

'I've – I've come to find your Pledge key,' she spluttered.

'My key!' Antonia said, pondering. 'How do you know about the key?'

'We know everything!' Elsa exclaimed. 'We know all about you – all about the Pledge! We know what you've been doing . . .'

Antonia tried her best to smile, but it was buried under years of plastic surgery.

'You've come all this way, all the way from the prison. What a brave little thing you are!' She threw her head back, laughing. Her neat black bob stayed perfectly still – Elsa wondered if it was even hair at all. From where she was sitting it looked more like a helmet.

When Antonia eventually stopped laughing, she turned to Elsa again. 'You must think it's wonderful, living a life of privilege. Let me tell you something. It's so frightfully boring! Sometimes I just sleep and I wake, not knowing whether it's night or morning, not knowing what day, what week it is. Worst of all is the feeling –' she paused – 'or the lack of it. I don't feel anything any more. Not joy, not sorrow.' She sighed.

Elsa placed her arms on the chair. She looked over at the glass doors to the garden. If she could get to the doors before the dogs, she might be able to escape.

'So, can I go now?' Elsa asked.

'Go? Go where, little girl?'

'Well, I can't stay here forever . . .' As she said this, Elsa seemed to shrink into her chair.

Antonia laughed again. 'Oh, you silly little thing. No, I'm afraid I can't let you leave. You need to go back, to the prison.'

'I'm never going back!' Elsa protested.

She sprang out of the chair and ran towards the doors. She had barely made it halfway across the room before one of the dogs tore towards her, trapping her against the wall.

'G-good boy,' Elsa stammered, not taking her eyes off the dog.

'Bring her to me,' Antonia said.

Just as the dog was about to pounce at Elsa, there was a *whomp* and the animal fell to the floor. Pyra pointed Elsa's ibis at the second charging dog and fired again, then at the third.

'My little angels!' Antonia cried, racing towards her pets. 'What have you done to them?'

'They're asleep,' Pyra said, pointing the ibis at Antonia.

Antonia let out a vicious scream and charged towards

her. But Pyra easily caught her, clutching the dressing-gown round her neck.

'You gonna talk to us about this key?' she said, holding Antonia at bay.

Antonia opened her mouth and bit into Pyra's hand, causing her to drop the ibis. Pyra yelled, nursing her hand.

Elsa bent down, grabbed the ibis and fired at Antonia's chest. The five-foot billionaire sailed backwards and flew into the wall.

'Get outside, Elsa,' Pyra said.

'Wait,' Elsa said, grabbing the sleeve of Pyra's leather jacket. 'What are you going to do to her?'

Pyra pointed to the garden. 'I mean it, Elsa. Meet me on the other side of the maze.'

'I don't want you to hurt her, Pyra. Please,' Elsa went on. 'We have to show them we're better than they are!'

'Then you'd better hope she gives up the key quickly,' Pyra said.

Elsa ran into the garden. A light snowfall had dusted the ornaments and was coating the frozen pond. She hurried to the maze and noticed a couple of broken branches arranged on the ground. *Pyra must've left them to help find her way back*, Elsa thought. The deeper she journeyed into the maze, the more branches she found.

It took almost fifteen minutes to reach the other side, where she was met with a field and the looming woodland up ahead.

Elsa sat down on an upturned log and checked her hand and arm. Although she hadn't noticed the pain, the dogs' teeth had punctured the skin and there were specks of blood.

Eventually Pyra emerged from the hedge maze too. She removed a key from her jeans pocket.

'So you got her to talk,' Elsa said, staring at the antique key.

'I'd never have found it if she hadn't,' Pyra answered. 'It was attached to one of those stupid dogs' collars.'

'And you didn't hurt her?' Elsa said, looking at Pyra suspiciously.

Pyra put the key back inside her pocket. 'I didn't *hurt* her.'

'Promise?'

'Yeah,' Pyra said. 'I promise. Happy now?'

They had just started to walk away when there was a shrill cry. Elsa looked back over her shoulder. 'That came from the maze,' she said, blinking away crystals of ice.

'Yep,' Pyra answered.

'You left her out there, in that? But it's snowing; she'll freeze to death!'

'The world will be a better place with her gone.'

Elsa tugged at Pyra's sleeve. 'We can't just leave her! You promised me you wouldn't hurt her!'

'And I stuck to my word. If she can't find her way out of her own damned maze, that's her problem. We'd never be able to find her in there anyway, would we?'

She said no more and walked past Elsa with her eyes lowered. Elsa looked at the hedge maze and in that moment she thought there was something quite wrong with the world, and people, and herself, as she finally turned away and reluctantly followed Pyra's fading footsteps.

30

Alyn opened his eyes and saw a figure sitting on the end of his bed.

'Hey,' Jes said.

'Hey,' Alyn whispered, squinting at her. 'What time is it?'

'About eleven.'

He groaned and sat up, wiping his hair from his eyes.

'Luthan wants us to leave soon,' said Jes, handing him a T-shirt.

'Right. Of course he does.' Alyn pulled it on and walked over to the window, rubbing his face with his forearm.

'Still don't trust him?'

Alyn shook his head.

'I still think you're wrong,' Jes said. 'There has to be an explanation. We should probably talk to him.'

'No. We don't say a word. Not yet, anyway.' He pushed away from the window. 'Just keep alert.'

Jes smiled sadly. 'You were always the idealistic one. The dreamer. The one to make friends . . .'

Now all I seem to make are enemies, Alyn thought. She didn't need to say it aloud. Alyn shrugged and reached for his boots. 'Yeah, well. I've been around a lot of bad people.'

Jes went back over to the door. 'Just try to remember there are some good ones too.'

Luthan, Alyn, Jes and Julian left the Guild's headquarters and took the car. Alyn sat in the back seat with Jes, staring out of the window. A couple of times he noticed Luthan drumming his fingers anxiously against the gearstick.

'Where are you taking us again, Luthan?' Jes asked.

'The docks,' he answered, looking at her in the rear-view mirror. 'Nover's supposed to be negotiating some kind of business deal there, according to our surveillance.'

No one in the car said much for the next twenty minutes, until Luthan turned the car on to an industrial estate.

'You got a plan?' Jes whispered to Alyn.

His eyes on Luthan, Alyn leant towards Jes to answer when there was a tremendous impact against the side of the car.

He was slammed into Jes, who was thrown against the door.

There was a black van driving beside them filled with men in dark clothing. The driver turned the van and it slammed into their car once more. 'Nover's men,' said

Luthan, struggling to regain control of the wheel. He spun the car round a corner, fleeing. The van turned after them.

Just then, Luthan's phone rang. Luthan picked it up.

'Still looking for me?' Stephen giggled. 'Thought I'd send some friends to give you my regards.'

Luthan ended the call and dropped the phone. The van behind accelerated into their bumper. Jes lurched forward.

'Might want to throw them off, Alyn,' Luthan said.

Alyn shut his eyes. 'I – I can't concentrate properly,' he said.

Jes reached between the seats and grabbed Julian's ibis. 'Open the sunroof.'

Luthan obeyed and then Jes unbuckled her seat belt and stood on the back seat, standing through the open sunroof. She squinted, trying to see through her blowing hair.

She aimed the ibis at the pursuing van and fired. The blast hit the window, which rattled but failed to shatter. The van swerved.

A man leant out of the rear window and fired with an ibis of his own.

Jes shot again, missing, and then a third time, causing a crack to appear on the van's window. She lifted the ibis again, looking along the barrel, her hair streaming wildly across her face.

With her final shot, the van's window exploded into a storm of swirling glass and the van veered into a wall.

Luthan slammed on the brakes and the four of them got out and hurried over to the crashed vehicle.

Luthan pulled out the driver, the only one who was still conscious. He fell out of the van on to his knees, whimpering under his breath. His face was covered with streams of blood from the broken glass. He tried crawling away but was lifted up by Luthan.

'You work for Nover,' Luthan said, slamming him on to the bonnet.

The man nodded cautiously.

'Where is he?'

'I – I don't know. He only gives us orders over the phone . . .'

'You're lying,' Jes said, pointing the ibis at his face.

'I've never even met him!'

Jes pressed the ibis against his throat. 'If you don't tell us right now, I swear I'll . . .'

'Chill out,' Alyn said, taking the ibis from her. He turned to Stephen's driver. 'Get out of here.'

The man looked at Jes, terrified, and sprinted away over the ice.

'The more pressing question is how he knew we were coming,' Julian remarked suspiciously.

'Yes,' Luthan said, peering at the unconscious men inside the vehicle. 'Anyway, we should leave. They'll probably be looking for our car.'

The three of them followed him in silence over to an alleyway between two rows of buildings. The ground was caked with grey slush. They emerged from the alley on to a yard, dotted with dilapidated-looking storage buildings, many of which were covered in aggressive graffiti. There didn't seem to be anyone else around, apart from a few seagulls.

'We'll lay low,' said Luthan. 'Make sure we aren't being followed. Then we can head back to base . . .'

Alyn waited until Luthan had taken a step in front of him, then said, 'No more games, Luthan. I know what you're up to.'

'Hmm?' When Luthan turned, Alyn was pointing the ibis at him.

'Alyn?' Luthan said. 'What are you –'

'I know what you've been doing,' he hissed. 'You're going to try to exchange us.'

'Exchange you?'

Without taking his eyes from Luthan, Alyn removed a pair of handcuffs.

'I took them,' he said. 'From your pocket.'

'Those were for Stephen,' Luthan protested. 'That's what we came here to do after all.' He looked at Jes and Julian. 'Come on, you two don't honestly believe this . . . ?'

'Out of everything that's happened to us, it's one of the more believable things,' Julian answered, sighing. 'Tell me, why were you going to exchange us? The Guild certainly seems to have enough money . . .'

Luthan shook his head. 'You don't understand.' He marched towards Alyn, his defensive tone turning into aggression. 'Just give me the ibis before you do something you regret.'

Alyn pointed it at his chest. 'I heard what you said to Stephen. I followed you.'

The shock was clear on Luthan's face. 'You *followed* me?'

Alyn nodded.

Luthan appealed to the others. 'I was trying to get close to Stephen. Like we're supposed to be doing now.' He gave a dismissive shake of his head. 'I don't have time for this.'

Alyn followed him with the ibis, until Julian stepped in his way.

'It was *me*,' Julian said. 'You were going to trade *me*. I only just escaped from Stephen's men. If Alyn hadn't warned me, I'd be back in the prison right now.'

'Nonsense,' said Luthan.

'No more lies,' Jes said, folding her arms. 'Tell us the truth.'

Luthan looked as though he was about to challenge her, but stopped and lowered his hands. 'If – if you must know, I wasn't doing it for power. Or for money . . . or to destroy. I was doing it for the man I love.'

Julian folded his arms. 'Things had been refreshingly unsentimental until now . . .'

'They'll kill him. I know what these people are like! Wouldn't you do anything to save the person you loved?'

Jes looked furious. 'You're telling me, you're putting us all at risk to save your boyfriend? You're risking *everything*!'

Luthan smiled weakly. 'I had no choice. Let's just

forget about it all and go back to our base. We can talk there.'

Alyn lowered the ibis. 'Wait here.' He pulled Jes and Julian away from Luthan.

'We can't let him go,' Alyn said. 'We need to keep him somewhere.'

'I don't trust him,' Julian whispered. 'Come to think of it, I've never warmed to him.'

'So what do we do – tie him up and leave him somewhere?' Jes looked uncomfortable with the thought. 'We should take him back to the base. We could tell the others, Pyra and Anton. They'd know what to do.'

Alyn shook his head. 'It's our word against his, and I know whose side they'll take.'

He looked up just as Luthan attacked. Luthan felled him with a punch and snatched the ibis out of his hands.

'Get back!' Luthan snarled. 'All of you! Get back!'

Luthan fired at Julian, catching his leg. Julian let out a cry and collapsed to the ground. Still dazed, Alyn scrambled to his feet.

Jes ran towards Luthan and threw a kick at his leg. He stepped away and fired at Alyn, who was charging at him. Alyn ducked and tackled him to the ground. The pair rolled until Alyn ended up beneath Luthan with the ibis in between them.

'Give up!' Luthan snarled, trying to secure his finger against the trigger.

Alyn managed to lever the weapon and squeeze the trigger instead. Luthan wheezed and passed out, tumbling backwards into a puddle.

Julian hobbled to his feet, using the chain-link fence to support his now-useless leg. 'That settles it then,' he panted.

Alyn pulled out the handcuffs again and looked around. He spotted a deserted metal storage unit a short way across the yard. 'In there,' he said.

He and Jes dragged the unconscious Luthan inside and handcuffed him to a forklift in the corner. Luthan murmured groggily.

'The Guild can bring him back later, if they want. I just want him gone.'

With that, Alyn reached up and pulled the shutter down. The pair went back outside, to find Julian limping towards them.

'He was doing it for *love*,' Jes said, shaking her head in disbelief.

'Mm. Surprised you weren't taken in,' Julian said to her. 'You being a girl and all. You love that kind of nonsense.'

Jes raised an eyebrow. She waited until Julian had limped a short way ahead before kicking his good leg from under him, sending him crashing down into a puddle.

31

Ryan and Anton watched as the cackling, red-faced Blythe waddled out of his Rolls-Royce. The pair were standing among a crowd of spectators, outside an orphanage that the Pledge member was due to open. A lilac ribbon was tied in a bow across the iron gates and fluttered in the freezing wind.

Ryan looked up as a red-haired girl walked past him. It wasn't Jes. He felt his heart sink.

'Don't worry,' Anton whispered. 'I'm sure she's fine.'

Ryan looked embarrassed and lowered his eyes. 'What's the deal with Pyra? I can tell you like her.'

Anton looked at Ryan then gave a disappointed sigh. 'She's not interested.'

'Well, what are you gonna do?'

Anton looked puzzled.

'I mean, aren't you gonna keep trying?'

'She's not some prize to be won. Hey, it's her choice at the end of the day. If she changes her mind some day, great. If not . . .' Anton trailed off. 'Anyway, why do you look so glum all of a sudden?'

A surge of guilt had filled Ryan's stomach. He had already tried using the Ability to change Jes's mind, to make her like him. He thought of Pyra's reaction when she had figured that out. She had been angry, furious even. He hadn't seen what the big deal was, but now, looking back, he knew it was wrong. After all, how would he feel if someone used the Ability on him?

'Nothing's wrong,' Ryan said, narrowing his eyes as Blythe pushed his way over to the gates. 'But we've still got no idea where his key is. Could be anywhere. Could be in a safe in another country for all we know.'

Anton shook his head. 'If there was a ton of evidence that might land you in prison for the rest of your life and one thing that might get rid of that evidence, where would *you* keep it?'

Ryan shrugged. 'Look, mate, I'm not a bloody detective . . .'

'You're not an idiot either. Come on, Ryan. Think.'

'Somewhere I could get to it easily enough, I suppose.'

'Exactly! Wherever that key is, it's going to be within reach. Anyway, he's about to speak.'

Ryan glanced over at Blythe, who was now standing in front of the gates with an oversized pair of scissors. He couldn't have looked less interested if he tried.

'Yes, yes, great honour to be here and all that. I declare this old people's home open,' he announced, moving towards the ribbon with his scissors.

'Sir, it's a children's home,' said his chaperone quietly.

'Hmm. Well, they'll probably be old too some day, won't they?' He chuckled, throwing a wave to the press, and stomped away.

'Man, this guy is some kind of idiot,' Ryan said, scowling. 'Makes you wonder how he got his money.'

'Inherited, of course,' Anton muttered. He watched as the drunk Blythe collided with a council member.

'Drunk at the opening of a kids' home,' said Ryan. 'Classy. If he weren't so dangerous, he'd be a joke.'

Anton sidled through the clapping crowd, followed by Ryan.

Blythe gave the crowd a final wave and disappeared into his car.

'Come on,' Anton said, hailing a taxi. He opened the door for Ryan and they hopped in. 'Follow that –'

'Wait,' Ryan said. 'Can I say it? Wanted to my whole life.' He leant towards the driver and pointed. 'Follow that car. Cheers, mate.'

A short while later, Blythe's Rolls-Royce pulled up outside a lofty Georgian townhouse. With an enormous amount of effort, Blythe climbed out of the passenger seat and waddled precariously towards the door.

'Here will do.' Anton leant forward and passed some money into the taxi driver's hand. The driver looked at the pair suspiciously and snatched the money from Anton.

Outside, on the pavement, Ryan said, 'So, we gonna break in or what?'

Anton nodded. 'But not yet.' He saw Ryan rolling his eyes in protest, then said, 'It'll be easier if he drinks himself into a stupor.' He checked his watch. 'Let's give him a couple of hours.'

'Suit yourself,' Ryan grumbled. He marched over to a small park nearby and sat on a bench with his arms folded.

Having not moved from the bench for the past two hours, Ryan was shivering. Anton had been pacing anxiously up and down the road with his hands in his pockets.

Ryan's thoughts soon turned to Jes again. If she had managed to find her family, there was a good chance she was staying there . . . lying in bed, wrapped up in some fancy quilt, while he was out freezing his backside off, waiting for some drunk rich guy.

He muttered to himself, driving his knuckles against the bench. Why couldn't he get her out of his mind? Sometimes, it felt like it was *her* using the Ability on him.

Maybe he should forget about this Blythe bloke and go looking for her instead. Then he remembered what his mother had said: '*Just come home, Ryan. And don't go being a hero.*'

Don't go being a hero. Funny she should say that. If it weren't for him leading them, none of them would've ever escaped the prison. Had any of them thanked him?

'Time to go, Ryan,' Anton said. 'Keep watch while I see to the lock.'

Ryan nodded and looked around the deserted road, shivering.

Anton crouched by the lock and began wiggling a piece of metal inside. Then he took another piece and began shifting it around. The whole scene made Ryan think of a dentist poking around in someone's mouth.

'It's open,' Anton hissed as the lock eventually clicked. He pushed the door gently, revealing the chequered floor of Blythe's hall. The sound of violins drifted through the air from a room above.

'You have to show me how to do that sometime,' Ryan said, impressed, and stepped inside.

32

It was evening when Alyn, Jes and Julian returned to the Guild's headquarters. A solemn mood had fallen upon the group as they ambled through pools of misty orange light from the streetlamps.

'And you all wonder why I'm so cynical . . .' Julian said.

Alyn tapped in the code for the security gate. 'Never thought I'd hear that coming from you, Julian. Let's forget about Luthan for now. And no word of this to anyone, right?'

Jes and Julian both nodded and passed through the gate behind him. At that moment a car arrived with Elsa, Harlan and the others.

Elsa was first out. 'Alyn?!' she exclaimed, then paused, hesitant to approach him.

'Hey, Elsa,' he said with a smile, throwing her a friendly wave.

Elsa looked to Jes, then back at Alyn. 'I – I thought you'd switched sides . . . I mean, I saw you, with Felix –'

'Never,' Alyn said. 'I'm with you guys. I always have been.'

Elsa rushed over and wrapped her arms round him.

Pyra patted Alyn on the shoulder. 'What made you come here?'

'You're going to need as much help as you can get,' Alyn said, then looked over at the car as Charlie lifted Harlan out of the back and hoisted him up in his arms. 'Harlan? Is he OK?'

'He's sick,' Pyra said, avoiding his eyes. 'He passed out on the way back.'

Alyn noticed the blood around Harlan's nose and unconsciously brushed a finger against his own.

'Is there something we should know about?' he said, turning to Pyra. 'Has this got something to do with *us*?'

Pyra shook her head. 'He'll be fine. He just needs to rest.'

The others sat at the dining table and talked among themselves, but Elsa went to her room, unable to concentrate. Saul, the man in the locked room, and Harlan were both sick. Even Alyn seemed worried that something strange was going on.

Elsa left her room and went down the corridor. When she was sure no one was coming, she removed the key from the skirting-board and went inside the bare room.

'Hello again,' she said, as her eyes began to adjust to the darkness and to the figure buckled to the mattress.

Saul's eyelids flickered. 'Ah. Child,' he answered. 'How good to see you.'

Elsa made sure the door was closed behind her and pulled over a chair.

'Look at you,' she said, shaking her head. 'You look a real mess, if I'm being honest.'

Saul smiled. His eyelids flickered.

'I haven't seen myself in months. They won't trust me with a mirror, you see. The sharp pieces. They think I might . . .' He trailed off, noticing the brush in Elsa's hand.

Elsa smiled and began brushing the tangles out of his long curly hair.

'Thank you, little one,' he said. 'Now, have you kept it a secret, like you promised?'

'Promise,' Elsa said. 'I want to ask you about this sickness you have. I think the same thing is happening to my friend, Harlan.'

'He's been overusing the Ability, hasn't he?'

'Yeah, actually. How did you know?'

'Because the Ability causes it, little one. Even you are in danger. We all are.'

Elsa stopped brushing his hair.

'I'm sorry,' he said. 'Perhaps I should've said nothing.'

Saul's breathing became suddenly shallow and his shoulders rose and fell.

'Saul? Saul, are you OK?'

'It's happening again,' he groaned.

'*What's* happening?'

'The pain,' he groaned. 'My mind . . . it feels like it's falling apart . . .'

A stream of blood trickled out of his nose, as his eyes rolled back.

Elsa's eyes filled with tears. 'I want to help,' she said. 'I just want to help you!'

'Kill me,' he whispered. 'Please, child, just kill me.'

33

Alyn sat beside Jes. 'Cheer up,' he said, touching her arm. 'We've still got time, right? We'll stop the Pledge.'

'It's not that,' she said. 'I just hope Ryan's OK. Pyra said she hasn't heard a thing from him and Anton.'

Alyn looked at her for a few moments. 'I'm sure he's fine.'

Jes tried to smile and got to her feet. 'I'll be back soon.'

'Where you going?' Alyn said.

'Outside. Just want to get some fresh air. It's been a long day.' She gave him a look that compelled him to stay.

He sighed to himself. 'Can't work you out any more. You're a mystery.'

He watched her leave and ran his fingers through his hair. Ryan had been the last inmate taken to the prison, and he and Alyn had never clicked. Alyn was a dreamer, Ryan driven by his temper. *Too reckless*, Alyn thought, but perhaps the real problem was that he saw too much of himself in Ryan. More than he would've liked.

'She'll be back,' Pyra said. Alyn turned round, not aware that she'd been watching.

Alyn managed a faint smile. 'How's Harlan doing?'

'He's resting,' she said vaguely.

'Not surprised he's ill with everything we've been through . . .'

'He's fine. He's just tired.' Pyra said nothing more and wandered to a noticeboard, looking at the pinned photographs of the Pledge. The photograph of Felix now had a black cross drawn over his face.

Deceased.

Alyn looked away, unable to shake the image of Felix lying on the ballroom floor, his blue eyes glazed and lifeless.

'So what was he like?' Pyra asked, plucking the photograph from the board. 'Felix, I mean. As evil as they say or just . . . ?'

'Misguided,' Alyn answered quietly.

'Misguided.' Pyra frowned. 'Sure I could think of a few other words to describe him. They wouldn't be repeatable.' She put the photograph back on the board and lifted the marker pen, and drew an X across Antonia's face.

'Two down.' She took a small blank piece of paper, drew a large question mark on it, and pinned it below the photograph of Stephen.

'That supposed to represent Emmanuel?' Alyn asked.

Pyra nodded. 'Guessing he doesn't have many pictures on the internet.'

Alyn got up, unpinned the question mark and placed it above Stephen.

As he walked past the window, Alyn saw a swarm of masked people climbing out of two trucks. A chill spread through his veins. 'Hang on,' he said. 'This doesn't look good.'

Pyra looked up.

Alyn shielded his eyes from the reflection in the window as Pyra came over. The figures had gathered and were standing in a semi-circle, just fifty metres or so from the building. A man wearing a dark overcoat stepped to the front and began to speak to the crowd.

Emmanuel, Alyn realized. *He's here. He's found us.*

34

Emmanuel examined his amassed followers as they stood opposite the Guild's building in the drizzling rain.

'As soon as the blackouts hit London, everything will descend into chaos!' he called to the crowd. 'But chaos is good. Chaos is change. Chaos is life. It is stillness that is death. And our society has been still for far too long.'

He walked slowly along the length of his followers. 'Our enemies want the old order kept. Our enemies are the enemies of progress,' Emmanuel went on. 'They must be crushed!'

The horde cheered, thrusting their fists into the air.

'We'll crush them!' yelled a man at the back of the group, raising his hand.

'Yes. We will,' Emmanuel declared. 'And we shall begin with a group of people who have been trying to stop us in secret like the cowards they are. They call themselves the Guild.'

He turned and pointed to the block of flats behind him.

'We will destroy them first, to send a message, a warning, to the others – to the men and women who rule this country. A message that we are coming for them!'

The gang roared, throwing hands and fists into the air.

'Take no prisoners,' Emmanuel ordered. 'Kill them all.'

'Who are they?' said an alarmed Pyra as she stood beside Alyn, looking at the jeering horde below. 'Are they Stephen's men?'

'Emmanuel's,' Alyn answered. 'He thinks you guys are going to stop the project at the prison before *he* can use it.' He pulled away from the window. 'I'll go down there. He knows me after all; I might be able to reason with him . . .'

Pyra grabbed his arm. 'Don't be stupid, Alyn. They're in a frenzy. They'll tear you to pieces.'

Alyn watched as the mob began moving towards the security gate. He noticed an array of weapons glinting in the lamp-post light, from bottles and clubs to metal bars and chains.

'As long as that gate is locked, they won't be getting in,' Pyra announced. She walked away. 'I'll tell the others.'

'I hope you're right,' Alyn said with some reservation, peering down.

Pyra nodded. 'Trust me, they'll never make it. Unless you have the code, it can only be opened from the inside.'

'We should call the police,' Alyn said, looking for a telephone. He spotted one on the far table and was just making his way towards it when the doors to the dining room swung open.

'I can't believe you kept him in there like . . . like an animal!' Elsa yelled at Pyra. Her face was red and covered in tears. 'And the same thing's going to happen to us!' she exclaimed. 'We're all going to get sick. We're all going mad!'

'What are you talking about?'

'Saul!' Elsa sobbed. 'He's sick, just like Harlan is!'

Pyra grabbed her by the shoulders. Alyn watched as the colour left her face; it was the first time he had ever seen her look truly scared.

'Elsa, what did you –'

Elsa pulled away from Pyra's hands. 'I let him go, you maniacs! I let him go!'

Alyn turned back to the window and spotted a dishevelled-looking man in a white nightgown limping clumsily through the crowd.

'*It's open!*' Alyn heard someone shout. He craned his neck and could just about see the security gate swinging gently on its hinge.

The gang outside surged together towards the now-open entrance.

Pyra set off towards the corridor, but Charlie grabbed her arm. 'Too late. You'll never get it closed in time.'

'What did I do?' Elsa said, looking at each of them in turn. 'I didn't mean to . . . I was just trying to help him.'

Harlan entered the room from the far corridor, rubbing his eyes. '*Alyn?*' he said, recognizing the face of his friend. He looked around the room at the others. 'What's going on?'

'We're under attack,' Julian answered.

Harlan looked to Alyn for confirmation. 'How many?'

'I don't know, maybe thirty.' Alyn panicked. He began looking around the room for something that could be used as a weapon.

Pyra grabbed Elsa by the arm and marched her towards the fireplace. 'Get up the chimney,' she said. 'The rest of you, who has ibises?'

'I left Harlan's in the car,' Elsa called over, halfway inside the fireplace. 'I'm sorry, I –'

'Never mind. What about you, Julian?'

'I have mine,' he shrugged. Against so many, the weapon was more or less useless.

'So just one.' Pyra muttered something under her breath and helped Charlie drag a table across the large double doors. They positioned it so that it was wedged, locking the handles in place.

Alyn raced back to the window. Outside Emmanuel and his assistant were standing together, looking up at the window in silence, while rain streamed across them.

Alyn leant out of the window.

'Hello again, Alyn!' Emmanuel called up to him.

'Call them off!' Alyn shouted down. 'Please! Call them off!'

'You know I can't do that.'

'We won't interfere with the project,' Alyn begged. 'I swear it!'

Emmanuel shook his head. 'We all know that if I let you leave, you'll come after me. You'll ruin everything.'

While Alyn tried reasoning with Emmanuel, Pyra found herself a weapon: a brass candlestick holder. She turned, noticing a nervous-looking Julian standing beside her.

'Thinking of switching sides, Julian?'

'Bit too late for that,' he answered. 'I'm not going anywhere.'

Wouldn't blame you if you tried, Pyra thought. She closed her eyes and took a deep breath. When she opened them, the door began to thud with the barrage of charging bodies. There was a split second of silence and then a thunderous crash as the doors buckled and finally broke under their weight.

35

After leaving Alyn, Jes had walked by herself around a deserted car park a short way from the Guild's building.

It was bitterly cold. Swirls of silver curled from her lips and her face stung from the chilling winds, which seemed to be tearing in all directions. Moments later, the soft patter of rain fell on the pavement.

With a sigh, Jes decided to return to the others. She jogged across the road and started back through the park towards the tower block. Upon seeing dozens of masked men streaming towards the building, she halted.

Something wasn't right.

Jes lowered into a crouch, hurrying from one car to the next to avoid being seen. She edged closer, her heart thudding.

Up ahead, she saw a man in a white night-gown cowering on her side of the road, shivering and distressed.

Using the parked vehicles to shield her from view, she hurried towards him. 'Hey,' Jes hissed, trying to grab his attention. The man looked up with wild eyes, startling her.

'Who are you?' she said. 'What's going on over there?'

'She freed me,' he whispered, tears running down his dirty face. 'The little girl, she freed me. It was all I wanted.'

'What little girl?' Jes asked in a whisper. 'Are you OK? You look –'

'No. No.' He gripped his head and flopped into a sitting position on the ice-covered pavement. 'I'm not OK. It's the Ability, you see . . . you must be careful . . . if only I'd known . . .'

'I don't understand,' Jes said. 'But I can try to get help. Just wait here and I'll be back –'

The man's breath rattled in his throat. 'It's too late. It's too late.'

His eyes rolled back and he fell forward, as blood trickled out of his nose.

'Hey,' Jes said, tapping his face. 'Wake up, please wake up.'

'I'm free,' he repeated softly. 'It doesn't hurt any more. Please tell that little girl Saul said thank you . . .'

He gave a final murmur and fell still. Jes opened her mouth to shout for help, but it was too late; he was already dead. She whimpered and backed away, looking up just in time to see the group rushing towards the open tower-block entrance.

My friends, the Guild, they're all inside . . .

A man in a black overcoat was standing outside the building, watching the ensuing chaos. *Emmanuel.*

She looked around for a weapon. There was nothing

except a squashed cigarette packet and a rotting banana peel.

Maybe if she had the Ability she might have been able to make something happen. But she didn't. She wasn't one of *them*. Instead, she would have to rely on less subtle methods to get things done.

'Guys, help us!' shouted Charlie. He and Pyra were leaning against the table in front of the door, struggling to keep it closed from their invaders. Julian ran to help, followed by Harlan and Alyn.

'What's going on out there?' Elsa yelled from the fireplace.

'Stay put!' Pyra shouted back. She turned to Charlie. 'Where are all the others? It can't just be us here . . .'

Charlie shook his head.

The door thudded again. The mob were breaking through.

'It's going to give!' Harlan cried. The doors burst open and a mass of bodies charged into the room. Charlie was knocked over by a swinging plank and staggered backwards.

Harlan tried to pull him out of the path of the swarming herd, but was grabbed and thrown towards the fireplace.

Quickly the room became a mass of brawling bodies. Alyn charged at a man and wrestled him to the floor, just as Harlan was climbing back to his feet.

When Julian's ibis was knocked from his hands, he

backed against the wall, watching the violence with a look of terror across his face. A large man wearing a gorilla mask approached him and threw a punch. Panicking, Julian ducked as the man's fist landed against the wall.

The man yelled, crumpling at the waist and clutching his fist. Julian launched a kick between his legs and hopped over his body.

Pyra jumped up and drove an elbow into a man's skull, then aimed a kick at a woman who was about to slam a steel bar over Harlan's head. She looked up as more people flooded into the room.

Even if the rest of the Guild somehow managed a last-minute appearance, they were completely outnumbered.

Jes moved silently towards Emmanuel. Her fingers twitched in anticipation, remembering the self-defence classes her parents had forced her to take last term. She took a breath, quickened her pace and threw herself at his back.

Emmanuel lurched forward suddenly, giving her greater momentum. She fastened her right arm beneath his throat and the other arm applied pressure to his head, choking him.

Emmanuel spluttered, trying desperately to throw her from his back.

'Call them off!' she snarled. 'Call them off or I swear I'll . . .'

She applied more pressure to his throat.

Emmanuel reached up, grabbing for her hair. His fingers found a chunk and he pulled, tearing a handful of hair from her scalp.

Jes yelped and tears flooded her eyes, but she held on through gritted teeth. Emmanuel continued grasping, clutching.

'I'll kill you!' she screamed. 'If you don't call them off, I swear I'll kill you . . . I've done it before and I'll do it again . . .'

He fell to his knees and made another attempt to grab her hair. She could feel his strength leaving him.

'There has to be a way to stop them. If you don't, I swear I'll . . .' She squeezed his throat tighter.

Wheezing, Emmanuel held a hand towards the building.

The street lights flickered. Jes stared at them in amazement. Then Emmanuel's hand dropped. Each of the surrounding lamps dimmed, as did all the lights in the tower block, draping it in darkness.

She unwrapped her arms from his throat and crawled away from his unconscious body, panting and clutching her side.

36

All light disappeared suddenly from the Guild's tower block, transforming the room into a pandemonium of tumbling shadows.

'Don't let them escape!' yelled one of Emmanuel's followers, turning back and forth and trying to locate the Guild in among the struggling shapes.

Alyn dropped to the floor and crawled to the window.

Had Emmanuel's plan already come to pass? Below he could see Jes limping towards the doors and an unconscious Emmanuel on the ground.

He turned away from the window and heard a familiar voice under the shouting.

'Let go of me!' Elsa shrieked. 'Help, someone, help! They've got me!'

Alyn scurried in the direction of the sound. He shut his eyes, feeling the familiar tingling sensation, snaking through his skull. Moments later, the man holding Elsa fell to the floor, unconscious.

Alyn felt for Elsa's hand and took her, pushing through the mass of bodies.

'Whoa, what did you do to him?' she whispered.

'It doesn't matter. You OK?'

'Yeah,' she said and squeezed his hand. 'I'm OK.'

'Alyn?' he heard Pyra say in the darkness. 'Is that you?'

Alyn felt for Pyra's hand and joined it with Elsa's. 'Take Elsa,' he said. 'Get the others. Get everyone out of here.'

'Since when did you start bossing everyone around?' Pyra snorted, but she grabbed Elsa's bony wrist.

'Since I became the leader of the Guild,' Alyn answered. 'Now go.'

37

In the moonlight from the parlour windows, Lord Blythe resembled a slumbering walrus, hauling thunderous snores. Surrounding him were several half-empty bottles of wine. A cheerful violin concerto chirped from the antique record player on the corner table.

'That noise is savage,' Ryan muttered, plugging his fingers inside his ears to block out the din.

'Shh!' Anton urged.

'Come on – he'll never hear us over that racket!' Ryan walked over to Blythe's chair. 'Wake up.'

Blythe continued snoring.

Ryan slapped him across the face. 'I told you to wake up.'

Blythe caught sight of the pair, gave out a terrified croak and fell backwards from his chair.

'Help!' he cried out, unable to climb to his feet. 'Help!'

'No good, mate,' said Ryan.

'Then take my money,' Blythe said, flustered. 'Take my home. Take anything. Take everything.'

'We don't care about your stinking money,' Ryan said, glaring at him.

'Then what on earth *do* you want?'

'A key,' said Anton. 'We know each of you has one. We're going to destroy the prison and end the project.'

'Who – who told you about that?' Blythe panted.

'Doesn't matter.'

Ryan ran up and kicked him in the stomach. Blythe wheezed and rolled back against the chair. 'You little ruffian!' he cried, trying to shield himself. 'Get off me!'

'That's for putting us there,' Ryan snarled. 'And this is for –'

Anton pulled Ryan away. 'He'll be no good to us unconscious.' He grabbed the fallen aristocrat by the shirt. 'We're ending the project, the Pledge. It all stops here, Blythe.'

'You want the key?' Blythe croaked, holding his stomach. 'Tough. You're not getting it.'

Anton stood. 'Fine. We'll do it your way.' With a tremendous deal of effort, he dragged Blythe over to the fireplace. The heat of the flames created a wave of sweat across his brow.

'Going to push me in?' Blythe cackled. 'You wouldn't dare!'

Anton steered him closer to the fire. Large damp patches were forming on Blythe's shirt. Drops of sweat rolled gently down over his brow and on to his ruddy cheeks.

'You'll never get the key,' Blythe wheezed, chuckling. 'My devotion is to the Pledge. To the greater good . . .'

Anton pushed him closer to the fire until Blythe was panting. 'I want that key, or I swear I'll do it . . .'

Anton's hands moistened with sweat as he continued to drive the billionaire towards the flickering flames.

'You'll never get the key!' Blythe hissed. 'Ever towards better things! *Semper ad meliora!*'

Anton eventually let go and walked away, across the living room. 'I can't do it,' he muttered. 'I can't.'

Blythe laughed, wheezing. 'You bloody coward!' he yelled, laughing. He rolled over, struggling to raise himself to his feet. 'I knew you wouldn't do it. You don't have the guts! You're pathetic.'

Ryan silenced the drunken billionaire with a kick to the face. 'I'm sick of the sound of your voice.'

'That's that then,' said Ryan, scratching his head as he and Anton stepped out of Blythe's house and into the falling snow. 'Bet *Pyra* would've got it out of him. Bet *I* could've done. You're too much of a nice guy, that's your trouble. If you'd have just given me five minutes alone with him . . . Matter of fact, I'm going back in there now.'

Before Anton could stop Ryan, the boy was already jogging back up to the front door. He was about to shove it open, when an elderly man in a tuxedo appeared.

'Who're you?' said Ryan, frowning. 'What do you want?'

'I'm Lord Blythe's butler,' the old man answered. He raised his hands submissively, as though afraid he might be assaulted. 'I was hiding beneath the table when you – when you . . . *accosted* him. I heard the whole thing.'

'What is this?' said Anton defensively, walking towards the pair. 'Some kind of joke?'

'No, no. I can confirm it isn't a joke, sir. Not at all.' He removed a small wooden box and handed it to Anton. 'I believe that this is what you're looking for.'

Anton opened the box. Inside was a key on a cushion of blue silk. He turned his eyes back to the butler. 'Why are you helping us?'

'Because I've been his servant – his *slave* – for far too long. He's a cruel man. A brute.'

Anton closed the box and locked the clasp. 'I'll make sure you're rewarded by our people.' He patted Blythe's butler on the arm.

The old man lowered his head gratefully. 'Take the key, whatever you need it for. That buffoon deserves everything that comes to him. Now, if you'll excuse me.'

With that, the old man gave them a parting nod and disappeared into the darkness.

38

Alyn, the other teenagers and the remaining Guild members regrouped in the park, away from their attackers. There was no sign of Jes anywhere; presumably she hadn't wanted to risk staying around. The group watched from the darkness as amber light flickered in the windows of the tower block. Someone had started a fire.

'Who was that man in white?' Alyn asked, nursing a cut on his forehead from one of Emmanuel's followers.

'He's my friend. His name is Saul. The Guild was keeping him prisoner!' Elsa said accusingly, looking at Pyra.

Pyra shook her head. 'He *wasn't* our prisoner. He was one of us. We were looking after him. Making sure he wouldn't hurt himself ... He was –' she paused – 'he was sick.'

'How did he get sick?' Alyn asked.

Pyra and Charlie looked at one another, before Pyra turned back to the group. 'All right, so we haven't been completely honest with you,' she said. 'You guys might want to sit down for this.'

'I'd rather stand,' Alyn said, feeling a rising suspicion. 'Just tell us what's going on, Pyra.'

Pyra sighed. She scratched the back of her neck. 'It's caused by the Ability.'

The group were silent for some moments. The wind roared noisily between them, strumming the branches of a nearby tree.

'You mean that's what's wrong with *me*,' Harlan said. 'It's not just some bug, or . . .'

Pyra shook her head. 'It's much worse than that, Harlan.'

'All the stuff you've been teaching us to do sends us mental, doesn't it?' Elsa challenged.

'Good job I haven't wasted my time then . . .' said Julian.

'Ever since the project started, the fabric of reality has been damaged,' said Charlie. 'And that damages *us*. Each one of us.'

'I think I'll take that seat now,' Harlan said, sinking back against a tree. He covered his face with his hands.

'Think of it like a whirlpool,' Charlie went on. 'The more you use the Ability, the more it pulls you towards it –'

'And once it's got you . . .' Pyra shook her head. 'It doesn't even matter if you stop using the Ability. It's too late. As long as the project at Nowhere is still going . . . and those kids are screwing with reality on such a scale, we're all gonna get sucked in eventually. We'll *all* get sick.'

Alyn felt like he'd just been punched in the stomach.

He turned to the others, who were silent and solemn with the weight of Pyra's words. 'So even if we stop the project we're still too late?' he asked. 'Is that what you're saying?'

Pyra shrugged. 'We don't know. But Henry thinks it's like a wound. We think that if reality has a chance to heal we'll be OK. We *hope*,' she corrected herself.

Pyra's words stayed with Alyn. He turned, walking away from the group and locked his fingers behind his head.

The only sound was Elsa, crying with fear, and the furious wind. Out of the corner of his eye, Alyn saw something blow on to the grass: a plastic snake mask that must have belonged to one of Emmanuel's followers. He scooped it up, then turned back to the group. 'I dropped Felix's key in the warehouse. I'm sure Emmanuel has it.'

'But we still need Nover's,' said Pyra. 'And we don't even know if Anton and Ryan had any luck getting Blythe's. I haven't heard a thing from Anton all evening.'

'If Emmanuel's already got his army on the march, we don't have long. It's going to be a matter of hours, not days ...' Alyn slipped the mask inside his hoodie. 'His followers are gathered in a park, a few miles south of here.'

'How do you know?'

'I've been in his base. I've seen maps, photos. Anyway, that's where I need to go, as soon as I've found Jes.'

Pyra stepped towards Alyn. Her eyes narrowed. 'Back at base you said you were the new leader of the Guild.

You want us to take you seriously, you'd better start backing up that claim.'

Alyn glared at her and left before she could say anything else.

'So, where are you taking us again?' said Elsa, hurrying beside Pyra as they walked down the busy street, snowflakes blowing into her face. Her hair was a tangled mess, flapping frenziedly. It seemed like they'd been walking forever.

'A safe house in Mayfair,' Pyra answered, not looking back at her.

'And, um, how *safe* is it?'

'No one else knows it exists,' Pyra replied. 'It's an abandoned underground station.'

'Oh of course it is,' Julian muttered. 'When you mentioned Mayfair, I thought swanky hotel ... but, alas, it seems you people are against doing anything normal ...'

'What's the fun in normal, Julian?' Pyra quipped. 'Try and keep up. We're still twenty minutes away.'

Elsa hugged herself to try to soften the vicious winds. 'How come you lot know about this place anyway?'

'The city is full of secrets, for anyone who cares enough to look,' said Charlie. He gave her an encouraging smile.

Elsa exhaled and looked over her shoulder at Harlan, shuffling some way behind. He was clutching his head.

'You OK back there?' she called to him.

Harlan looked up blankly and nodded. 'I'm fine.'

'Not far,' Pyra said, stopping momentarily to gather her bearings. Elsa noticed a bruise on her cheekbone and several cuts on her face. 'Luthan will meet us here as soon as he sees the base.'

'Ah. Hate to be the bearer of bad news but Luthan won't be coming back,' Julian said.

Elsa turned to face him. 'What?'

'We *detained him*,' Julian said. 'We were going to tell you earlier, but we thought you wouldn't take it well. And then there was the part where we almost got massacred by a gang of bloodthirsty maniacs, so . . .'

Pyra grabbed Julian's shirt, pulling him towards her. 'What are you talking about?'

'He was going to exchange one of us and give us to Stephen!' Julian spluttered. 'When I say "one of us", I mean "me", but I –'

'You're out of your mind. Why the hell would he do that?'

'To use the project to save Henry . . . his boyfriend . . .'

'Hey, if this is another one of your stupid jokes, Julian . . .' Elsa said, trying to stop Pyra from hurting him.

Julian held his hands up. 'It's fine. He's safe. But, if this Emmanuel character has his army on the move, I – I just thought you should probably know . . .'

Pyra tightened her grip on Julian. 'You're going to take me to Luthan so we can bring him back.'

'How? You don't have a car. Otherwise we'd be in it

now, rather than trudging on foot through this arctic weather . . .'

Pyra grabbed Julian's coat. 'For your sake you'd better remember the way, Julian.'

She turned down a vacant side street, scooped up a brick, then walked over to a parked car. She slammed the brick through the window and reached inside, unlocking the door. 'Charlie, take Harlan to the safe house. I'll meet you there as soon as I've got Luthan.'

'Sure thing,' he said, and put an arm round Harlan, leading him away.

'Wait, I'm coming with you two,' Elsa said to Julian and Pyra. She gave a sheepish Julian a disappointed look before following after them.

39

Emmanuel massaged his throat with his fingertips. It was still sore from where the girl had grabbed him less than an hour ago. Surrounding him were several hundred of his followers, all still masked. Scattered fires burned in bins around the vast expanse of snow-covered fields. Only the lights from the distant buildings gave any indication that they were near civilization at all.

'Sir,' said his assistant, clambering towards him. 'I'm so glad to see you, I got separated –'

Emmanuel looked down at him. 'My orders were for you to stay with me. Where were you?'

'I'd gone up with the others, sir. I didn't know you wanted me to –'

'He was hiding,' said a voice from the crowd.

'Hiding? *Hiding?* No, sir, that's not true, I swear I –'

'We saw him, sir,' said another masked man.

'I saw him too,' another agreed. 'He's a coward . . .'

'I gave you the privilege of being my right-hand man,'

Emmanuel said. 'And you have failed me. Tell me the truth and you might be forgiven. Continue to lie to me, however . . .'

The nervous man looked at the surrounding crowd. He turned, attempting to push through them, but was caught and pulled back into the centre.

Emmanuel advanced with a piece of rope. 'Hold him down.'

The assistant was taken down to the ground, kicking and struggling. Emmanuel grabbed his foot in mid-air and tied the rope round it. He threw the other end of the rope to a man sitting on a motorcycle.

'Sir!' the man begged. 'Please, I swear I'll –'

Before he could finish, the motorcycle engine roared and he was dragged across the cold snow and slivers of hard ice in the grass, flapping and flailing his arms. The group watched in silence as the motorcycle tore to the left and on to the unforgiving tarmac path.

Once the screams had faded into the distance, Emmanuel turned back to his followers.

'I expect nothing but your full devotion. Your commitment. Give me this and I promise you'll be well rewarded.'

'You want us to start looking for that girl who attacked you, sir?'

Emmanuel nodded. 'At once.'

'And what do you want us to do?'

'Don't let her take her own life.' He scowled. The

ferocity in his voice was cruel and simmering with hatred. He tossed a branch on to the fire that was burning near his feet, causing a sudden flash of flame. 'When the girl realizes what I have in store for her, she'll have no other choice. I want her to suffer.'

40

After he had left Pyra and the others, Alyn set off to find Jes. He walked through a quiet council estate, looking left and right, and calling out her name.

In the distance a noose of smoke frothed around the Guild's tower block as a wail of fire engines pierced the silence.

'Jes?' Alyn called out again. 'Jes, it's me.'

Moments later, Jes stepped out from behind a wheelie bin and flashed him a relieved smile.

Alyn jogged towards her. 'You OK?' He brushed his fingers through her damp, tangled hair and against her cold cheek.

She nodded. 'Yeah. I'm fine. But Emmanuel's gone.'

'I know,' he said. 'I need to get Felix's key from him. I just wanted to find you first. The others have gone to some abandoned station; it's some kind of back-up base ...'

'I don't care where they've gone. I'm coming with you.'

Alyn shook his head. 'I need to do this alone.'

'No, Alyn.'

Alyn grabbed her by the coat. 'I mean it. If he catches you, he'll . . .'

'I don't *care*,' Jes hissed, pushing him off her. 'Who are you to tell me what to do anyway? I'm sick of you trying to protect me, Alyn. Always the same story – when we were back in the prison you'd given up; you didn't want me doing anything. But who saved you all just now? Me. I made Emmanuel cut the power back at the Guild building. But you still don't trust me.'

Alyn shook his head and walked away. 'You'll get yourself killed.'

Furious, Jes marched towards him. 'Or he will,' she said.

Alyn grabbed her and kissed her and she put her hands against his face, pulling him towards her.

'I've proved myself by now, haven't I?' she said.

Alyn felt Jes's fingers link round his. He kissed her back and felt like his breath had left his chest. For a moment, the weight of everything lifted from him: Emmanuel, the Pledge and the sickness. None of it mattered. The two stood there silently in the middle of the deserted street.

The snow glowed ochre beneath the street lamps. Flakes drifted through the hazy showers of light, flowing like sparks.

'Come on,' Alyn eventually said, as reality began to intrude upon them. 'Let's do this. Together.'

*

Half an hour later, they arrived at the park gates. Shrouded in darkness, the pair were just able to make out figures standing around as the mist seeped in between the trees.

Alyn took the snake mask from his pocket and gave it to Jes. 'Here,' he said. 'Just in case.'

As they neared the park, they became aware of a couple of police officers standing nearby.

'Wouldn't go near there if I were you,' said one of them. 'There's something going on. Some kind of gathering.'

'Why haven't you done anything?'

''Cause *they* haven't,' said one of the police officers. 'Not yet anyway. But we're keeping an eye on things, don't you worry. First sign of trouble and we'll be there, with plenty of back-up.'

Jes and Alyn released hands and walked through the gates. Large numbers of people were standing around, talking, watching, illuminated by the light from scattered fires.

'Jeez,' she whispered to him, slipping on the mask. 'How many are there?'

Alyn shook his head. 'There seem to be more all the time.'

'Let's split up,' he whispered, pulling up his hood. Jes nodded and walked away over the grass, quickly mingling with a smaller group.

It was as she left him that Alyn paused, pinned to the spot. *You could go back. You'll never be able to reason with him.*

He looked back at the gates. It would be so much easier to turn round. To just leave and forget it had ever happened – to let things unfold. Maybe Emmanuel was right. Maybe they – the Guild and his friends – were wrong. Emmanuel wanted change, and perhaps so did everybody else.

Maybe change is what is needed.

But this wasn't just change, Alyn thought, studying the horde. This was opening the door to anarchy, and once that was unleashed even Emmanuel would be powerless to control it. Homes would be burned to the ground, people – *innocent* people – would be attacked and robbed. Whether Emmanuel wanted it or not, the weak would inevitably perish.

Reluctantly Alyn continued on, and as he journeyed further into the park, he began to notice little canvas tents dotted around, belonging to the more devout of Emmanuel's followers. Their leader had to be nearby.

'Hey,' said a voice beside him. Alyn turned as a man in a lion mask stepped towards him. 'Who are you?'

'I'm looking for Emmanuel,' Alyn said.

The man laughed, stepping closer to Alyn. 'You can't just *demand* to see him,' he said. 'It don't work like that.'

'He knows me. And I have something he wants.' Alyn held the man's eyes. 'And if you don't let me see him he'll want to know why.'

Alyn pushed past the man and spotted Emmanuel a short distance away, standing in front of a leaping fire.

Alyn closed his eyes and took a deep breath. He walked closer, aware of eyes following him.

Emmanuel eventually looked up. 'You just can't keep away, can you, Alyn?'

He took a step towards Alyn. A circle of his followers instantly formed around them.

Alyn could feel his hands trembling. 'I've thought about what you said. I want to do an exchange.'

The surrounding crowd made an excited mocking sound.

'And what do you think gives you the right to ask for an exchange, *boy*?'

'I'm no boy,' Alyn said. 'I'm the new leader of the Guild.'

Emmanuel walked closer towards him. 'Is that so?'

'I've done what you asked,' said Alyn. 'Luthan is yours. He's handcuffed in a storage unit a few miles from here.'

'And what do you want in return?'

'Something I dropped. It belonged to Felix.'

Emmanuel removed the key from his coat. 'This?'

Alyn nodded. 'Yeah. That's it.' His heart began to race.

Emmanuel smiled menacingly. 'Why?'

'It . . . it opens a safe,' Alyn lied. 'There's money. Felix promised me it as . . . as compensation. I want it.'

Emmanuel turned the key over, examining it carefully.

'If you're going to unleash chaos, I want to make sure my friends and family are able to survive,' Alyn went on, furthering his lie. 'We can't stop you.'

Emmanuel shook his head. 'This is what it's all about, Alyn? Money?'

Alyn walked towards him and reached for the key but Emmanuel pulled his hand away. 'You really think I would give it to you that easily?'

Two men grabbed Alyn from either side before he could reply.

Alyn shut his eyes. He imagined a butterfly fluttering through each man's skull, into the grey matter, setting off a sequence of synaptic flashes as a gentle prickling sensation snaked through his own.

The men released their grip, flopping on to the grass.

Emmanuel smiled with a look of what seemed to be respect, as another three men rushed forward.

'Let him go,' Emmanuel said, and put the key back inside his pocket. 'If his word is good, the key is his. Get Luthan's location from him. I want some people there to verify it at once.'

Alyn looked around at the circle of animal masks. He could see threads of vapour rising past the plastic; he could hear the rattling crackle of breath. His eyes followed Emmanuel as he walked away with Felix's key tucked safely in the pocket of his coat.

41

Ryan and Anton sat on a rattling bus on their way back to the Guild's building. Ryan had been staring at the key for the last few minutes. Such a fuss for something so . . . *stupid*. He just hoped they were right, that together the keys triggered some explosive device at the prison which would put an end to the project once and for all. Then he could finally go home.

He was sure his mum would have a heart attack when she saw him there. *Just come home, Ryan. And don't go being a hero.*

The bus slowed and Ryan followed Anton and jumped off. It was only when he looked up that he noticed a spiral of grey smoke billowing like a wreath above the Guild's tower block.

'Hang on, is that coming from –'

'Our building,' Anton said, quietly, staring at it in silence for several seconds. The pair ran across the road, narrowly avoiding the oncoming traffic, and sped across the park to a chorus of honking horns.

'What's going on? What happened?' Ryan cried as

they neared the building. He spotted a fireman and ran towards him.

'Please step aside, sir,' the fireman said, pushing past.

'My friends and I live here,' said Anton. 'Please, I need to know –'

The fireman looked sympathetic. 'I'm sorry. We think it was probably an arson attack. Is there anyone you'd like us to –'

'Were there bodies?' Anton said. 'Was anyone hurt?'

The fireman shook his head. 'As far as we can tell there were no bodies.'

Ryan pulled Anton to the side. 'Who do you reckon it was?'

'I don't know,' Anton answered, still staring at the building. 'But I know where the others will be.'

Forty minutes later, Ryan and Anton arrived at the disused station in Mayfair. Anton tapped the boarded door in a secret entrance at the rear.

'Hey,' he said. 'Anyone here?'

'Anton, is that you?' a voice answered.

'Yeah. I'm with Ryan.'

The door opened and Anton sneaked inside, followed by Ryan, who looked around the candlelit space. It was an old station, all right; he could make out the shape of a ticket office and a rusted London Underground sign on the wall. There was an old table, a couple of chairs and a floor covered with sleeping bags. On the walls were faded, torn posters and plaques. Ryan made a fist and sneezed. The entire room smelled of soot and ash.

Preferred the other place, Ryan thought. At least there he had a bed. This looked like something out of a bloody horror film.

'Someone gonna tell us what happened?' Anton said.

'Emmanuel happened,' Harlan replied. He was holding a tissue beneath his nose to try to stem the flow of blood.

'Where are the others?'

'Pyra went with Julian and Elsa to look for Luthan,' said Charlie. 'Alyn went after Emmanuel. I'm guessing Jes is with him.'

Jes and Alyn. Ryan felt his stomach tighten. *Alyn is back. And he's with Jes.* He removed Blythe's key from his pocket, knelt down and placed it on the floor.

Harlan picked up the key. 'Well done. If Jes and Alyn manage to get Felix's key from Emmanuel, that means we just need Stephen's.'

'And an instruction manual,' Ryan quipped.

Harlan examined the key carefully, then suddenly gripped his head. 'It's happening again,' he whispered.

Charlie grabbed his arms, trying to hold him still. Harlan's eyes rolled back in his head.

Anton hurried over to help Charlie. 'Whoa, has he got the.–'

Charlie nodded. 'The same thing that happened to Saul.'

Ryan looked horrified. 'What's happening to him? Is he having a fit?'

'We call it the sickness.'

'The sickness? What do you mean? Like food poisoning or . . . ?'

Anton looked solemn. 'It's caused by the Ability. It happened to one of our people, Saul. In just a week he'd got so bad we had to tie him up, for his own safety. He lost his mind.'

Ryan looked to Charlie. 'Tell me he's joking, right?'

Charlie continued watching Harlan. 'He's telling the truth. Saul said it was like being in a constant déjà vu. Then the déjà vu would keep getting worse and worse until his mind couldn't take it and he'd pass out.' He nodded to Harlan who was delirious, muttering things under his breath, as if to prove his point.

Ryan stepped away. 'No way.'

'We're all at risk, Ryan.'

'Man,' Ryan said, turning away. He covered his face with his hands. 'Why didn't you tell us this might happen?'

'You think it would've helped?'

'No, but –' Ryan shook his head and squatted against the wall – 'Never mind.' He looked up to see that Harlan was now unconscious, his face glistening with sweat.

'I'm gonna find Jes,' Ryan said, jumping up and heading towards the door.

'No,' Anton said. 'We need you here.'

'No offence or nothing, but I want to find my friends.'

Anton walked towards him. He put a hand on Ryan's shoulder. 'If we're attacked, we'll go down fighting. We need you here, Ryan.'

Ryan let out an exasperated sigh. He turned back from the door and slammed a fist into a corrugated sheet of metal on the wall.

42

Pyra spun the steering wheel and turned sharply into a poorly lit industrial-looking road.

'You *sure* Luthan's down here?' she said.

Julian pretended to ponder. 'A loaded question with many philosophical implications. Can anyone really be sure of anything . . . ?'

Pyra gave him a filthy look.

'Yes I'm sure,' Julian muttered and folded his arms.

Elsa popped her head in between the front seats.

'And I don't know why *you* had to come,' Pyra said.

'I wanted to help!'

'Help? Help with what exactly, Elsa?'

Elsa shrugged. She didn't really know herself. She sneezed, still dusty from hiding in the chimney.

'Park here,' Julian said.

The car bounced on to the kerb. Pyra kicked the door open and dashed out.

Julian followed her out and hurried over to the chain-link fence. 'He's in there,' he said, pointing to a grubby, metal storage unit. 'I'm going to hold back, if you don't mind. We didn't exactly say goodbye on a happy note.'

'Nice try, but you're coming with me. Now get over.'

Pyra shoved Julian towards the fence and climbed up swiftly behind him. Elsa waited on the other side by the car, looking anxious.

'On second thoughts I'll come too,' she said, leaping at the fence. 'I don't want to wait here by myself.'

Once at the top, Julian rotated and tried to descend, but slipped and landed on the gravel. Pyra grabbed him by the back of the coat and hoisted him up. 'Lead the way.'

Julian trod carefully across the icy ground towards the unit, while Elsa followed behind them, looking over her shoulder. She wished they could hurry up and find Luthan; something didn't feel right.

'I still can't believe you all did this,' Pyra hissed, stomping after him.

'He was going to trade us. He didn't give us much choice.'

Pyra shook her head in disbelief and pulled open the doors. The unit was empty, apart from a forklift in the corner with a single broken handcuff hanging from it.

She turned to Julian. Julian offered her a blank shrug.

'You think they got to him first?' Elsa said, looking worried. Neither Pyra nor Julian answered. Elsa gave a sigh and left the storage unit. She froze, noticing a pair of car headlights, sweeping beams of milky light across the compound. Something spiked in her stomach, a sense of dread.

'Julian, Pyra,' she hissed. 'I think we need to get going . . .'

The car stopped and a gang of four men got out, dressed in bomber jackets, with their faces covered. 'The kid said he was here,' Elsa heard someone say. 'Come on.'

They marched towards the fence. One of the men removed a pair of bolt cutters and began prising the lock. It soon snapped and the gate fell open. The group headed into the yard and towards the empty storage unit.

Elsa hurried back to the others. 'Guys, we need to get out of here,' she said. 'Run!'

Julian and Pyra glanced over their shoulders, spotting the gang enter the empty unit.

'Get to the fence on the far side,' Pyra hissed, moving quietly on the balls of her feet, so as not to alert them. The three ran towards the fence, Elsa trailing, looking back over her shoulders.

'I'll never get over it in time!' she whispered, staring up at the fence. 'I'll hide. You guys go.'

The gang were just emerging from the empty storage unit. Pyra grabbed Julian's arm, shoving him at the fence. Elsa looked left and right and darted behind some wooden pallets.

She watched as Pyra and Julian started to climb the wobbling fence. *It's always me left behind*, she thought. *The weak one. The slow one.* While their building had been attacked, what was she doing apart from hiding in a chimney?

'Either the kid was lying or we're too late,' she heard one of the men say.

'Wait a minute,' said another. 'Look. Footprints.'

Elsa looked down at the ground. The footprints in the slush led directly to her. It was only a matter of time before they found her.

Elsa stood up. 'I swear I didn't do anything!' she spluttered. 'I got lost. I was looking for somewhere to sleep and I went in there, but that's all . . .'

'She's coming with us,' one of them growled. 'The boss was looking for some girl who attacked him, wasn't he? Least we won't be going back empty-handed.'

He and another man grabbed Elsa and carried her towards the car. She tried calling out to Pyra and Julian, who were some way from her by the far fence. But it was already too late.

43

Alyn walked alone through the park, watched by Emmanuel's followers. Wherever Jes was, he hoped she wouldn't try anything stupid before Emmanuel's men returned with Luthan.

He looked left and right, trying to pick her out among the display of grotesque animal masks when a sudden noise from the path caught his attention: a faint groaning sound.

A short way from him a man was lying on his back clawing at the air. His foot was attached by a rope to a motorcycle that was parked beneath a tree. The skin had been torn from his face and his shirt was shredded.

Alyn gasped. Only when he knelt down did he realize the figure was Emmanuel's assistant.

The gravel and ice had done such damage that he resembled a burns victim.

Alyn knelt down and helped him stand. The man promptly collapsed again, sending them both tumbling on to the damp grass.

'You,' he groaned weakly. 'You did the right thing.'

'Huh?'

'He's a bad man,' the assistant continued. 'He's dangerous. You were right to tell him to get lost.' With that, he passed out.

Alyn lowered him back down and looked up as a car drove through the park's gates and tore across the grass. Alyn hurried across to a tree and darted behind it. He watched as the car parked and the figures got out, carrying a struggling girl.

She tried to call out, but a hand across her mouth muffled her cry.

Elsa.

Jes patrolled the park in secret, slipping in between groups of Emmanuel's followers, who were standing or sitting around on the grass with their faces hidden. Snow had started falling again lightly. She felt traces of sweat forming around her nose, beneath the thin plastic mask.

More than once she noticed the masked figures looking at her, as though they had detected she was an intruder – and she felt her heart seize in her chest. She lifted the mask halfway, wiped her face with her sleeve and continued on.

There was some commotion coming from the centre of the largest group. Jes craned her neck. A girl was being carried along by a man and a woman.

Emmanuel appeared in front of the fire. 'So, this is my attacker?' he said, eyebrow raised. 'You're . . . smaller than I expected.'

Jes pulled back behind the tree. *He doesn't realize it was me.*

'I swear I didn't do anything!' she heard Elsa cry. 'I don't know what you're talking about!'

'Even if it wasn't you, you're still part of the Guild.'

'The who?' Elsa stammered, attempting to lie. 'Never heard of them!'

Emmanuel placed his hand inches away from her head. 'You have the Ability, girl. I can feel it.'

He said something quietly and Elsa was lifted and thrown to the ground. She began kicking and screaming as a rope was tied round her foot.

'Someone fetch the motorcycle,' Emmanuel ordered. 'I'm going to see her punished.'

Jes ran out. 'Please, let me do it, sir!' she shouted from behind her mask. 'I – I want to punish her.'

'Enthusiasm,' Emmanuel announced to his followers, gesturing to Jes. 'That's what I like to see.' He nodded and Jes sprinted off, wondering what she was going to do next.

44

The boy at the front of the classroom tried to stand, but found himself too weak. He sank back into his seat and watched vacantly as a pair of guards walked over to the teacher, who had been sitting to the side of the projection screen.

'We need to know what's going on,' he heard one of them say, not bothering to lower his voice. 'Something isn't right – I mean, look at the kids –' He gestured at the room.

The inmates had been forced into watching the same film, played over and over, in shifts. Almost every inmate in the room was bleeding from their nose. Many had succumbed to unconsciousness; others were on the verge.

'I have my orders and you have yours,' she answered, not bothering to lower her voice. 'Return them to their cells and bring the others in for the next shift.'

'But they're not even learning anything, they just –'

'He's right,' said another guard. 'This is completely mad.'

'What part of *orders* don't you understand?'

The boy watched the guard reluctantly make his way to the door. 'Come on,' he said with a sigh. 'Get back to your cells, everyone.'

The boy eventually managed to stand and followed the line of others to the door. There was a peculiar feeling in the room: a hazy, pulsing sensation that seemed to be sucking him towards it. The inmates weren't the only ones who felt it, though – the guards did too. He could see it on their faces.

He and the other inmates left in a line, while the rest were ushered in to take their place. They shuffled along the walkway, drooping and defeated.

'Inside,' the guard said to him, pointing to his empty cell. The boy froze, looking at the thin mattress. A few hours of sleep and then it would be back to the classroom again.

'I can't do it,' the boy said desperately. 'Please, I can't do it any more. I feel sick.'

'Get in.' The guard grabbed him and threw him across to his bed. 'Next shift starts in six hours. Try to get some rest.'

The boy scrambled up and ran to the cell door, but the guard quickly locked it. He dropped down, resting his forehead against the bars, and closed his eyes.

When he looked up again, he noticed his cell light was beginning to flicker.

45

Stephen arrived at the restaurant surrounded by a fleet of bodyguards, all virtually interchangeable men: bulky and sullen with shaved heads and neck fat spilling over their suit collars. He pushed through to the front of the queue and the maître d' hopped out from behind a lectern. 'I'm sorry, sir, but there *is* a queue . . .'

'Don't you know who I am?' Stephen sneered at him.

'No, I can't say I do, sir . . .'

'Then take a guess!'

The maître d' looked at Stephen's solemn bodyguards. 'Um, a pop star?'

'Pop star!' Stephen giggled. 'Maybe some day. We shall see.'

He sauntered through, as the maître d' chased after him. 'Sir, do you have a reservation?'

'Yes. *All* of these seats are mine. You might as well tell everyone else they're going to need to find somewhere else to eat, because quite frankly I don't want them anywhere near me. In fact, I don't even want to look at them.'

*

A short while later, Stephen was seated alone at a table in the middle of the enormous Art-Deco-inspired restaurant. He delicately attached a napkin to his suit and glared as a nervous young waiter fumbled with a match to light the candles. Once he'd succeeded he turned to Stephen, lowered his head and said, 'Sir, I would like to inform you that today's specials are –'

'Are you educated?' Stephen interrupted, gazing vacantly at the leather-bound menu.

'I'm sorry, sir?'

'*Educated*. Are you educated? Do you have an education?'

'Well, yes, I suppose I –'

Stephen sighed, rolling his eyes. 'What are you educated *in*?'

'I-I have a degree in politics,' the man stammered.

'And here you are, serving the richest man in the country. How fitting. A fine politician you'll make some day!' He giggled and tossed the menu on to the table. 'Bring me the soup.'

'Sir.' The waiter nodded and hurried quickly from the table.

Stephen drummed his fingers impatiently, casting a look at his army of surly bodyguards seated in twos at little tables around the restaurant. He smiled at how bizarrely intimate they looked, then removed his phone from his pocket and dialled a number.

'Rayner,' he said quietly. 'I haven't heard anything

from you recently. I want to make sure that ghastly woman has been obeying my commands, as discussed . . .'

'This isn't Rayner,' said a voice on the other end. 'Who is this?'

Stephen looked puzzled. 'Who are you? This is Rayner's phone.'

'*Was* Rayner's phone. We found him in the forest. His neck was broken . . . who am I speaking to?'

Susannah, was Stephen's first thought. Whatever had happened, she was behind it. He had grown to increasingly distrust the woman, especially after the fuss she had made when he had revealed his plans to her. Without Rayner to oversee her, there was nothing stopping her from using the project against *him. Yes*, he thought. *That's what she's going to do*. She had to be stopped, at once.

'Sir, your starter has arrived,' said the waiter as he placed a bowl of soup on the table.

With a swift motion, Stephen swatted the bowl away, hurling it across the table and on to the floor. The bowl shattered.

Stephen nursed his hand and got to his feet, watched by his obedient bodyguards who stood up instantly. 'How quickly can we get to Scotland?' he said.

'We could take the helicopter, sir, but in this weather it'd be a –'

Stephen grabbed the man round the throat. His delicate, manicured hands squeezed his assistant gently. 'I don't want to hear your excuses about the weather, or any other nonsense,' he hissed. 'Take me. *Now*.'

46

'It's no good, Pyra,' said Julian. The pair stood a short way from the storage unit. 'We've got no idea where they've taken her.' He pulled her away from the chain-link fence.

'We can't just leave her,' Pyra snapped. 'God knows what they'll do to her . . .'

'Alyn's gone to find Emmanuel,' Julian answered. 'There's no way he'll let anything happen to her.'

Pyra slammed her fist into the fence. 'You'd better be right.'

'I usually am,' Julian said. 'We can't save Elsa. But we still need to get Stephen's key.'

Pyra turned, sighing. 'I'll speak with the others. We'll arrange something.'

Julian shook his head. 'I'm not wasting any more time, Pyra. I'm going now.'

'Julian –'

'I'm through with waiting, Pyra. I'm going after Stephen.'

*

Pyra and Julian drove across London to Stephen's skyscraper. Rain filled the sky, lashing down in great swathes, fizzing against the concrete and turning the remaining troughs of snow into slush.

'It's all shut up,' Pyra said, giving the main doors a shove when they arrived.

Julian took Stephen's stolen swipe card from his pocket. He had taken it back from Luthan, just after they tied him up.

Julian ran the card across the box and the revolving doors opened. The pair walked through the deserted reception area to the lift.

'SIGIL,' Julian muttered, looking at the list of companies on the board. 'Top floor. Of course.'

They stepped inside and the lift rose swiftly in silence.

'It's starting to feel like the end,' Pyra said, gazing at her reflection in the mirrored wall.

'The end,' Julian murmured beside her. 'Yeah. I suppose it is.' He mustered as much of a smile as he could but said nothing more.

The lift soon pinged and the pair stepped out. They walked along the darkened corridor searching for Stephen's office until a whirring sound roared suddenly from above.

'A helicopter,' Julian said. 'He's here.'

The pair ran up the remaining flights of stairs and came out on the roof.

The helicopter was waiting on a landing pad. The

force from its blades blew Pyra and Julian's hair over their faces and hurled beads of water across the roof.

Julian crept out and crawled behind an electricity generator. Just as Pyra sneaked beside him, a solitary slim figure emerged from another stairwell and scurried over to the helicopter.

'There he is,' Julian whispered, watching Stephen closely. 'You take care of the pilot and anyone else inside the helicopter, but Nover's *mine*.' He gave Pyra a strained smile, then climbed out from behind the electricity generator, blocking Stephen's path.

Stephen stopped. 'You. *Again*. You're becoming quite the pest . . .'

Julian charged at Stephen and launched himself at the billionaire's waist. Stephen fell backwards and squealed, trying to claw Julian's eyes.

'I want the Pledge key,' Julian said, shaking Stephen. 'Give it to me!'

Stephen gave a sudden twist somehow, and managed to hurl Julian to the side. The two wrestled on the roof in the rain, struggling, pulling and grabbing at one another.

'Give up!' Julian yelled. 'We're going to end the project . . . We're going to destroy the prison . . . You're finished!'

Stephen shrieked, trying to free himself from Julian's grip. As he turned to the side, a button tore on his shirt, revealing the Pledge key hanging round his neck.

'I've got it!' Julian shouted to Pyra, who had just

thrown the pilot out of his seat and delivered a spinning kick into his chest.

He reached down, grabbed the key and tore the gold chain away from Stephen's neck. The key flew from the chain and landed in a puddle.

With Julian distracted momentarily, Stephen opened his mouth and bit down into Julian's ear.

Julian screamed.

Stephen lifted his head, mouth frothing with blood, and spat half of Julian's ear into the streaming rain.

Pyra looked up on hearing Julian's cry. 'Julian!' she cried, watching as a frenzied Stephen dived in for another bite. But the boy moved out of the way at the last moment and Stephen tripped, staggering towards the edge of the roof.

Julian reached out as Stephen fell, catching his hand. He slammed against the roof edge, with the young billionaire dangling hundreds of metres above the street below. Julian squinted as the freezing wind blew up at him. His ear felt like it was on fire and he could feel the cold trickle of blood on his neck. He was tempted to release his fingers and let Stephen fall, but something kept him holding on.

Julian reached down with his other hand, clutching Stephen's slender wrist. Once his grip was secure, Julian began trying to hoist him back on to the roof. But then, just as his fingers found Stephen's diamond-covered watch, the clasp broke.

Stephen slipped out of Julian's grasp like silk and spiralled silently through the rain to the street below. What struck Julian the most was that the young billionaire had not shown any fear or sorrow. He had not screamed. He had not even made a sound.

Julian sat mutely for a moment and gingerly touched his ear. His fingers came away blood-red.

He could feel a surge of emotion building inside him, of feelings that had fused together: the lightness of relief, the pity of his pain, the guilt and shock of Stephen's eyes meeting his before he fell to his death. The emotions rose through his chest and caught in a knot in his throat, choking him.

'You OK?' he heard Pyra say beside him. Her voice seemed a hundred miles away.

Julian nodded, biting his lip. He looked at Pyra and saw the sympathy in her eyes and his face broke. Tears streamed down his cheeks. It was the first time he had cried since his parents died.

Pyra knelt beside him. She put her arms round him and squeezed him. 'It's OK, Julian,' she whispered. 'Everything's OK.'

When Julian had finished sobbing he crawled over to the key. 'We did it,' he said, turning the key over in his hands.

'*You* did it, Julian,' Pyra replied. 'You did it.'

47

After finding the motorcycle leaning up against a tree, Jes rode it back across the park towards the large group by the fire.

If it wasn't for her father owning a similar bike and letting her ride with him, she might not have known what to do at all. *Thank God for his mid-life crisis*, she thought.

Elsa was silhouetted in front of the fire, held down by two of Emmanuel's followers. One of them was tying a rope to her foot.

'Help me!' Elsa yelled, kicking her legs frantically. Tears rolled from her eyes. 'Help me, someone, help!'

Jes parked the bike in front of the group. She looked down at Elsa, willing her to recognize her green eyes behind the mask.

'Take her for a little ride around the park to warm her up,' Emmanuel said. 'After her face has got used to the grass, take her on to the gravel.'

'Yes, sir,' Jes said, watching Elsa struggling with her captors.

'Stop right there!' came a cry from the trees. In all the commotion no one had noticed the police car driving into the park. Its flashing blue siren gave a single indignant blurt.

Emmanuel's followers moved swiftly in front of Elsa as the car slowed.

Two police officers climbed out. 'I don't know who you people are or what you're doing here, but enough is enough,' said one of the men. 'Who's in charge of all this?'

Emmanuel walked round from behind the fire with his hands raised. 'My apologies, officers,' he said. 'But I can assure you nothing untoward is occurring here.'

'Who are you?' said the police officer, looking around at the masked group. 'Are you protesters or something?'

The group was silent, apart from Elsa's muffled cries behind them.

The officer pushed a few members of the group aside and saw Elsa gagged and bound on the grass, trying to free herself.

He removed his radio from his belt, but before he could say a word a high-pitched wail filled the air. A pulse trembled through each member of the gathered crowd. Swarms of confused birds flew up and disappeared into the black sky, giving nothing away except the beating of several hundred wings. The surrounding street lights flickered then went dark, and all of the light was sucked out of the nearby buildings –

a ripple effect, one after the other – until there was nothing but a panorama of impenetrable darkness.

'Sir,' said the man nearest to Emmanuel, in awe. 'The power . . . It's all gone . . . The whole city is blacked out . . .' He turned to Emmanuel, eyes wide. 'Your plan has worked.'

'Hello?' the police officer said, jabbing his radio. 'Can you read me?'

'He can't,' Emmanuel said, as the crowd surged towards the powerless police officers.

As the officers were buried under a barrage of howling, yelling bodies, Jes hurried over and pulled Elsa to her feet. 'Elsa, it's me, it's Jes,' she said, raising her mask. 'Get on the bike.'

A little shaky and still sobbing, Elsa scrambled on to the rear of the bike, struggling to free herself from the rope.

'That sound,' she said, sniffing. 'Look, there's no power anywhere. Everything's gone black.'

'I know,' Jes said quietly, wishing that there was some other explanation but unable to conjure one. Emmanuel's plan had worked, and his next step was to tear the city to pieces.

She revved the engine and the pair sped off together through the park.

48

Alyn waited on the outer edges of the park, watching Emmanuel and his followers leave.

'Alyn! Over here!'

He turned, scanning the darkness. Elsa and Jes were waiting on the motorbike.

'Emmanuel still has the key,' he panted. 'I didn't get it. He's gone. I don't know where to.' He stopped. 'We were too late.'

'Come on – let's go after him,' said Jes. 'We can beat him, Alyn. I know we can.'

Alyn was about to speak but noticed a trickle of blood dripping from Elsa's nose.

'Elsa,' he said.

Elsa checked her fingers and turned pale. 'It's happening to me too,' she panicked.

'You must stay with the others,' Alyn said. 'Jes, there needs to be someone who doesn't have the Ability – who *isn't* going to be affected.'

'I want to come with you,' Jes said. 'I want to fight.'

'You need to keep hold of the Pledge keys,' Alyn said. 'If we lose them, this will all be for nothing.'

Before he had even finished, Alyn could see the desperation in her eyes. 'I need to find Emmanuel.'

He stepped close to Jes, kissed her on the cheek and left before she had a chance to change his mind.

49

Three days later

The Prime Minister was sitting in darkness inside the Westminster hotel, illuminated only by flickering candle flame. He lowered his pen, filled his glass with port and looked out of the window at the empty street. Ever since Felix had approached him and told him the Pledge's plan, he had been plagued with nightmares. *It is madness*, had been his first thought. Using a prison full of children with some *Ability* to change reality? Felix claimed they could transform the economy, solve military conflicts, halt terrorism. Foreign relations? Yes, Felix had answered. No problem at all. Health scares? Weather disasters, like the floods that seemed to be growing increasingly out of control? The project is like Aladdin's lamp, Felix had joked. *More like Pandora's box*, the Prime Minister now thought.

Now where was he? A shell of a man, haunted and hunched over a table in his hotel room. His therapist had told him he needed a holiday; he'd only been back a week, and in that time some of the inmates had escaped. He could feel the noose tightening . . .

There was a knock at the door. He jumped, releasing his pen. He leant down to retrieve it, but froze.

Another knock.

He cautiously got to his feet and shuffled towards the door. 'Who is it?'

'A friend.'

The Prime Minister paused. He felt his hand reaching down and turning the handle, as though he had no control over it.

'You,' he hissed, as Emmanuel stepped inside.

'I've come to relieve you of your duties,' Emmanuel replied. He gestured to the darkness around them both. 'No power. A fitting end to your reign.'

The Prime Minister walked over to the window and gazed at the streets below, which were covered in broken glass and debris. At the far end of the road a car was burning. A group of forty or so looters charged on to the street.

'Revolution by anarchy. It won't be the first time someone's attempted it. Nor the last, I imagine.' The Prime Minister sighed, shaking his head. 'There's one thing I've come to realize in all of this. Nothing's perfect. There is no such thing as Utopia. Someone's always better off, someone's always worse off. You may very well take control of the country, but you'll see the same problems emerging too, I promise. And you'll be in my shoes and another more dangerous maniac will have taken your place.' He took a sip from the glass of port on the table. 'Best of luck. You'll need it.'

'I appreciate the concern,' Emmanuel said, and plunged a blade in between the Prime Minister's ribs.

50

There was a cry, hoarse and desperate, and the scuffle of shoes on stone.

Alyn turned the corner and found himself confronted by a surging bonfire in the middle of the street. A row of shattered, dented cars were askew on either side of him. Shops and homes were boarded up, either as a result of their windows being smashed or to prevent it happening.

'Animals, animals!' came a voice at the end of the road. Alyn moved closer, keeping tight to the wall. A gang of rioters stood around in a circle, their faces covered by farmyard masks. A pig stood next to a lamb.

The lamb, the most threatening, gripped a suited man with one hand, while a knife danced close to his throat. 'You trying to say something, politician?'

'Only – only that the world's gone mad,' the suited man whimpered, staring at the knife.

'Mad?' said the man in the lamb mask, pushing him to the ground. 'No. This has been coming for a long time. You really that stupid?'

The man on the ground wheezed. 'I have no say in any of it . . . I have no say . . .'

'Makes two of us,' said the lamb. He pulled his victim to his feet and threw him on to a car. 'Which were you?'

'Pardon?'

'Which one were you – Eton or Harrow?'

'I don't know what you're –'

The man behind the lamb mask laughed. 'Did you have a servant? Silver spoon? You flabby, useless old –'

'Eton,' the man spluttered reluctantly. 'But that's not my fault, I –'

'Not our fault where we were born either. And we have the likes of you – a jellyfish – leading us. Making decisions for us. Taking control of our lives.' He twirled the knife tip against the man's tie, watching as the sweat descended his brow.

'Stop!' Alyn yelled, unable to contain himself any longer.

The group in animal masks looked up. The pig picked up a plank of wood and slowly walked towards Alyn, who shifted to the side, embracing the wall.

'Stop? You want us to stop?' said the masked man, creeping closer.

Alyn shut his eyes and visualized a butterfly. His head pulsed with pain; it was getting harder and harder to use the Ability. Alyn had started having the nosebleeds, along with feelings of dizziness and a constant uneasy sensation of déjà vu. It wouldn't be long before the blackouts started and the sickness claimed him. Maybe it had already claimed the others, his friends.

As the smiling pig mask stepped into view, Alyn stood taller.

The man lifted his plank of wood menacingly. Behind the eye slots, Alyn could make out two glistening eyes.

Alyn took a step back. The man in the pig mask took a step after him, but was slammed against the bonnet of a speeding car. There was a cracking sound and a bump, and the body was launched into the air, hit the ground and rolled across the tarmac.

Alyn turned and ran as fast as he could.

51

Elsa lit a match and lowered it to the oil lamp. She held it against the wick and sighed. Ever since Emmanuel had taken the power from the city, she and the others had been living in the dingy disused underground station. It reminded her of being back in Nowhere. Right where they'd started.

In just three days the city looked like it was in the aftermath of a civil war. Homes were burned, windows shattered and shops looted. Cars were left abandoned, where their owners had fled in panic.

There was still no sign of Alyn, and Elsa had already resigned herself to the fact that the worst might have happened. But Alyn was not the only one she feared they might not see again; the sickness had affected Pyra, Anton and the rest of the Guild far worse than her and her friends. They'd been using it for longer, after all.

It won't be long before it takes hold of me too.

'Here, Pyra,' Elsa said, passing her a mug filled with water.

Pyra murmured softly as Elsa put a hand behind her head, lifting her gently.

'Is it over?' Pyra whispered. 'Are things back to normal?'

'Almost,' Elsa replied.

A lie, but a comforting one. Elsa put the lamp down and went outside to join the others. It was snowing silently. The sky was white and she could make out the faintest hint of the sun struggling through.

Ryan and Jes were sitting together against the wall.

'It's been days,' he said. 'We've still not got anywhere close to Emmanuel –'

Elsa gazed at the keys. Antonia's, Blythe's and Stephen's were placed next to each other on the ground. *So close*, she thought. But without Felix's – now Emmanuel's – they may as well have none.

'And we still don't know what to do with them,' Julian interrupted. He had been listening to their conversation in secret, in that unnerving, careful way of his. Even he was beginning to look sick, tired and pale.

'He's making his way around the city,' Jes said. 'Trying to get all the rioters on his side. Seems to be working.'

'Someone always profits from chaos,' Julian murmured. 'Still, he must have an army by this point.'

'It doesn't matter,' said Jes. 'We've got to attack. We have to.'

'With what? We lost the ibises.'

'With whatever it takes,' Jes said, and got to her feet. 'We're not going to make anything happen sitting around. Come on, I mean, you guys have the Ability, right?'

'But each time we use it now we'll end up more like –' Elsa nodded over to Harlan, who was unconscious.

'But the same thing will happen if we don't,' said Julian.

It's true, Elsa thought. The Ability was the only thing that could both save or destroy them.

'So we're screwed either way,' Ryan said.

'Exactly,' Julian replied. 'Seems to be quite the recurring theme with us, doesn't it?'

52

The shadow of the Prime Minister's hanging body swung back and forth behind Emmanuel. A crowd of nearly a thousand had gathered and were watching intently.

Since the fall of the city Emmanuel's was not the only group that had attempted to seize power from the chaos. But, unlike the others, they were the only ones with a clear leader who was determined to take control and stop at nothing to achieve it.

Gradually, as if by sheer force of will, Emmanuel found the number of his followers increasing, pulled into his orbit.

'These people,' Emmanuel said, gesturing to the swinging body, 'our *government*, have led us into ruin. They've cowered away from the financial sector, let them get away with murder, and who suffers? Not them, the wealthy politicians. Not them, but *you*. The people. While they retire to their second or third homes, laughing at you all, it is *you* who are struggling to survive.' He paused, watching the crowd. 'They have led you into wars from the comfort of their expensive leather armchairs. Their necks are not on the line. They never have been. And, worst of all, they tell you that *you* are the problem. It is not you. It is *them*.'

The crowd cheered.

'We will purge the city of every last politician, every last liar and cheat and thief. And then we will take the financial district. We will burn their churches of money to the ground until there is nothing but rubble and glass. It begins at six o'clock this evening.'

Alyn watched from the crowd, his hood over his eyes. *What are they going to do tonight?* He thought back to Emmanuel's warehouse and remembered the crates of explosives. *The Houses of Parliament?* It would be a symbolic act to show that they had won . . . that law and order had been overturned.

'Join us!' Emmanuel cried. 'Let us eradicate this disease for good.'

Emmanuel raised his fist and there was another cheer from the crowd. He turned and left the platform, followed by a group of five people with their faces covered.

Alyn slipped through the crowd of spectators after him and it was then that he spotted Julian and Elsa lying in wait.

He watched Elsa hop up and throw a rock at one of Emmanuel's aides, knocking him back.

'Up there!' someone shouted.

There was a sudden rattle of gunfire, which caused the crowd to disperse. Alyn dashed behind a car and waited with his back against it.

'Hey,' came a voice.

Alyn turned to find Ryan standing just metres away from him. A broken piece of wood was clutched in his raised hand.

'Ryan,' Alyn said, getting to his feet. 'What are you guys doing here?'

'Same as you,' Ryan said. 'Trying to get the last key . . .'

'Trying to get yourselves killed, more like. All of you need to get the hell out of here. You've ruined everything, I was going to –'

Ryan scowled at him. 'You might think you're the leader of the Guild, but you ain't my leader.'

'You're attacking an armed gang with rocks and –' he looked at the plank in Ryan's hand – 'and bits of *wood*! Stop being such an idiot.'

Ryan stepped closer to Alyn. 'An idiot? At least we're trying. What are you doing? You've disappeared. No one even knew you were still alive . . . Jes has been worried sick . . .'

A man in a lion mask caught sight of the pair and hurried towards them. Alyn closed his eyes, gave a flick of his hand and the man slipped on a patch of ice, landing with such force that his body crumpled in the middle.

Alyn clutched his head, wincing. 'Jes,' he repeated. 'Is she OK? Where is she?'

'Dunno,' Ryan said. 'She's around somewhere. Anyway, I'd better get going.'

Alyn called him back. 'Wait. If you see her, I want you to tell her I love her. In case I never get the chance.'

Ryan looked at Alyn for a few moments, then at the ground.

'Ryan, will you –'

'Yeah, yeah, all right. I'll tell her. Look, we need to get going.'

Alyn watched Ryan swing the plank at one of Emmanuel's guards and hurry back to join Julian and Elsa.

'Where's Emmanuel?' Ryan said.

'He's already gone,' said a disappointed Elsa. 'Come on – we need to get out of here.'

53

Ryan trudged along as the Guild made their way back across the city. Litter from upturned bins blew around his feet. The smell of smoke filled the air.

He looked over his shoulder at the sound of footsteps and noticed Jes some way back.

'There's nothing we can do,' he grumbled. 'Even with the Ability. He's just got too many people. We can't get near him.'

He stopped talking and leant against a wall, holding his head.

'My head's killing me,' he groaned. 'If we leave it much longer, I won't be going home. That's all I want, to get back and see my mum. She needs me, she does. I promised her.'

Jes said nothing and he was glad; sympathy would've only made him feel worse.

'I'm worried about Alyn,' Jes said. 'I mean, he said he was going after Emmanuel, but I didn't see him there. I –'

Ryan looked at her, then down at his feet. 'I just saw him.'

'You did? When?'

'Back there. I spoke to him.'

'Why didn't you say something? You mean, you let him go off all by himself?'

He shrugged. 'Didn't have a lot of choice. It was pretty crazy.'

'Well, what did he say?'

Ryan was about to recall Alyn's words, but he stopped himself. 'Nothing much.'

'Oh.'

'Didn't say anything at all really,' Ryan went on. 'Think he's happy just being alone for now. You know what he's like.'

He took a step closer. 'Remember when you left?' he said. 'Remember how you kissed me?'

'Ryan . . .'

He put his hand against her face and Jes let it stay there for a few moments.

'I can't,' she said, and pushed it away. 'Not now, Ryan. I'm sorry.'

'Alyn . . .' he murmured, answering the question he hadn't even asked.

Ryan had tensed his fist to try to influence her again. But at the last second he closed his eyes and released his fingers. 'Jes?'

'Yeah?'

'He said . . . he said to tell you that he loves you.' The moment the words left Ryan's lips he pulled his hood up and jogged on ahead, leaving her standing by herself in the street.

54

'I don't know how much longer I've got left,' Harlan whispered to Elsa, not long after they had returned to the abandoned station. 'But I want to help. I want to *do* something.'

He looked terrible, even worse than when they'd left him earlier that day; dark rings hung beneath his eyes and his cheekbones were gaunt and hollow. His head sank back against the wall, unable to muster the energy for defiance.

'Look at you,' she said. 'You're a mess. You're not going anywhere.'

'Please,' he croaked. 'I can't stay here . . . just let me go.'

Elsa watched him sadly. She realized how the Guild must have felt having to restrain Saul the way they had.

'Remember how we didn't have any money or anything when we got to London? Remember how we were living on the streets and you were always trying to take care of me?'

Harlan nodded. 'Yeah,' he whispered, trying to smile.

'Well, it's my turn to take care of you now. And if you don't stay put I'm gonna get mad and you don't want that, Harlan . . .'

Her voice trailed off as she wiped a trickle of blood from her nose. The sight of blood had always scared her, but now she was used to it. The weakness and headaches were increasing, as well as the sense of déjà vu – reality was slipping away from her.

Elsa looked over at Julian, hoping he might have an answer. But he too seemed to have lost something in the past few days, as well as the top of his ear.

'I miss you being mean to me,' Elsa said, nudging him.

Julian looked at her blankly.

'You know what else I'm missing? Home.' She leant her head on his shoulder.

Jes sullenly entered the room, stepping over the quilts and sleeping bags.

'Any news?' said Elsa, getting to her feet. 'Any sign of Emmanuel? Any idea where he might be going next?'

Jes shook her head.

'Hey, come on, not you too,' Elsa said. She reached into her bag and removed the bubble mixture. 'Remember this?'

She held it towards Jes and blew a stream of bubbles in her face. 'Who needs technology when we have bubbles, right?'

Before Jes could muster a response, Ryan burst into the room.

'Guys, come outside,' he said. 'There's something you should see.'

Elsa, Julian and Jes followed him out and along the slush-filled alleyway.

'Wait,' he said, halting them before they came out on to the street. Elsa, who was directly behind him, peered out. A man in a bomber jacket wearing a giraffe mask was standing in front of a house, looking left and right. A piece of paper fluttered in his hands.

'One of Emmanuel's men,' Elsa whispered. 'He looks lost.'

'You think he might give us some information?' said Julian.

'Exactly. If we can make him talk –'

'We'll make him talk,' Jes cut in, then added, '*I'll* make him talk.'

Elsa couldn't help but admire her confidence, but kept her eyes on the man. This was far too good an opportunity to waste.

Ryan started creeping out slowly. At that moment, the man in the giraffe mask turned and saw the group. 'What you kids looking at?' he said. 'Gonna mug me or something?'

Ryan and Julian ran towards him. Elsa shut her eyes and whispered her locus under her breath as the others chased after him along the street. The man looked over his shoulder at his pursuers when a window swung open off the latch, hitting him directly in the face.

Elsa opened her eyes and hurried over to the others.

She could see why Harlan had got so addicted to the Ability.

'Good job, Elsa,' said Julian with a hint of his familiar sarcasm returning. 'Though he won't be saying much. He's out cold.'

'Hey, I'm sorry!' Elsa protested. 'I can't control exactly what happens . . .'

Ryan leant down and pulled the mask from the man's head and shoved it inside his hoodie.

Elsa leant down and plucked the screwed-up piece of paper from the man's hand. It showed a map of the Houses of Parliament with a number encircled:

$$18:00$$

She passed it to Jes.

'So that's where they'll be this evening,' Jes said. 'We should go.' She paused and her eyes filled with worry. 'This is probably our last chance . . .'

Elsa was glad Jes had said the words, so she didn't have to. Judging by the look on Ryan and Julian's faces, they were thinking the same thing.

'Before all this happened, I spoke to my mum on the phone,' Ryan said. 'I told her everything.'

Jes rubbed his arm encouragingly.

'The night they took me I asked my mate Carl if he thought we'd ever get somewhere in life. If we manage to pull this off, I reckon I have. I reckon we all have.' He looked down at the ground, as though suddenly embarrassed by his confession. 'That's about the soppiest thing you'll ever hear me say.'

'Here's to getting somewhere,' said Jes, reaching down and holding Ryan's hand.

55

A large crowd had gathered on the bridge and the grass beneath Big Ben when Alyn eventually emerged. He peered up at the tower and the silent clock; it had not chimed since the anarchy. There was no sign of Emmanuel anywhere. He left the bridge and went on to the grass, weaving through the crowd.

'It's about time,' Alyn heard someone beside him say. 'I've been waiting for this for years. I mean, I always knew there would be a revolution. I just never thought it'd be this good.'

A few of the others murmured in agreement and Alyn felt something curdle in the pit of his stomach. Of all the things that Emmanuel had used the Ability to manipulate, the public reactions were one thing that he *hadn't*.

And then it became clear: *people actually wanted this to happen*. They were sick of exploitation, of the authority of the greedy, the cruel and the corrupt. Emmanuel had merely been the architect of something that had been festering beneath the surface for decades. Perhaps even centuries. *Emmanuel was right.*

Alyn felt smothered by the realization and found it hard to breathe. He started to push away through the crowd, but a cry stopped him in his tracks.

'Here he is!'

Emmanuel climbed out of the back of a van, surrounded by a dozen of his followers. The crowd cheered as he made his way across the grass and stood before them.

'My friends!' he exclaimed. 'Today we burn, we destroy, and we rebuild!'

There was another cheer from the crowd. Three men were pushed towards the front. Two were dressed in suits, the other in a robe. Each had a bag over his head.

'Politician, banker, priest,' Emmanuel announced. 'The three tentacles of oppression. Of *the old way.*' He gestured to the man beside him, who led the captives to a low wall overlooking the River Thames.

Two of Emmanuel's followers grabbed the nearest man and hoisted him over the wall and into the river. Moments later, the second man was thrown in, and finally the third. Alyn drew in his breath in shock. A few of the people surrounding him looked away, but then there was a cheer, a trickle of laughter and an encouraging shout, then silence.

'The disease must be cut out of the city,' Emmanuel announced. 'And we won't stop until we have torn out every trace.'

Emmanuel's eyes searched the crowd. Alyn lowered his head and slipped through the mass of bodies. He watched as three men began carrying bags of explosives from a wooden crate inside a parked van. Another stood a short distance away, holding a flaming torch aloft.

Alyn felt someone tapping his shoulder and turned to find Luthan standing behind him. His hands were tucked into the pockets of his overcoat and a scarf was wrapped round his mouth.

'Luthan?' Alyn said, struggling to hide his surprise. He felt himself quickly becoming wary.

Luthan lowered the scarf with his forefinger and thumb. 'I came to say I'm sorry for what I tried to do – what I did. I've come to try to make amends. To make things right.'

'Get lost.' Alyn turned away, but Luthan's hand steered him back.

'You want them all taken out?' Luthan said without lifting his eyes from the group.

'I don't know what I want,' Alyn said, looking around at the enthusiastic audience. 'I don't know any more. I'm starting to think all of this was meant to happen. *Needed to happen.*'

'Maybe you're right,' Luthan whispered. 'But *this* man is not the one to do it. He's already threatened to destroy all of us. And your friends. It's only a matter of time before he succeeds. We have to stop him, Alyn.'

Alyn closed his eyes. All he could see was Jes, smiling back at him.

'I can help you take out his followers,' Luthan whispered. 'But then you need to deal with him. *Alone.*'

56

Jes, Julian, Elsa and Ryan emerged from Westminster Bridge just in time to see the final man be thrown over the side into the river. Elsa gasped and buried her face against Jes's coat. She heard Ryan swear under his breath.

'He's getting more followers by the day,' Jes said, watching the crowd. 'Almost as if the people want this . . .'

'Course they don't. They're only doing it cos they're scared,' Ryan answered, shoving his hands in his pockets. At least he hoped that was the reason. He closed his eyes, pinching his nose with his forefinger and thumb as pain stabbed between his eyes.

Jes put her hand on his arm. 'You feeling OK?'

He nodded. 'It's just my head. I'll be fine in a minute.'

'Look over there,' Elsa whispered. 'What are those people getting out of that van?'

'Explosives,' Julian answered. He checked his watch and added sarcastically, 'I was wondering when they might show up.'

Ryan reached into his hoodie and removed the giraffe mask he had taken from Emmanuel's gang member earlier.

'I reckon I can get inside it,' he said, his eyes fixed on the van.

'And?'

'And, while his lot are distracted by me, you guys can attack.' He looked down at the rusted pipe in Jes's hands, then back at her and grinned. 'You've beaten him once already anyway. I reckon you can do it again. In fact, I *know* you can.'

Jes smiled at him. 'Only problem is, his men are all armed. We won't last a minute against them.'

'No,' Julian suddenly realized, and nodded towards the van. 'As long as we're in there, we're safe. They'd never be so stupid to open fire on us while that cargo's in the back.'

Ryan nodded. He slipped on the mask and turned to Julian. 'Come on. Let's go.'

He and Julian hurried through the crowd together to where the van was parked on the grass, in the shadow of Big Ben.

Ryan tapped at the window.

The driver looked down. 'What?'

'There's smoke coming out of the back,' Ryan said. 'You might wanna have a look, mate.'

The driver shoved the door open and climbed out, just as Julian swung a pipe at his head. Ryan climbed inside, followed by Julian, who went round to the passenger seat.

'Now what?' Julian said.

'I'll head straight for Emmanuel. That should get their attention.'

He turned the key in the ignition and the van began rattling slowly across the grass.

That joyriding came in handy, he thought, feeling a little smug behind his mask.

Alyn watched in silence as Luthan pushed his way to the front of the crowd.

'Emmanuel!' Luthan shouted. 'That is your name, isn't it? Very exotic.'

Emmanuel stopped talking and watched as Luthan walked towards him.

'You wanted me, didn't you?' He pulled the scarf from his face. 'Here I am.'

'Luthan,' Emmanuel said, 'I was expecting the Guild to make an appearance sooner.' He gestured to some men carrying a small box of explosives. 'Bring him to me.'

The pair lowered their crate on to the grass and grabbed Luthan, dragging him towards Emmanuel.

Alyn looked at the crate and shut his eyes. *An explosion. That would do it. Especially if Emmanuel was in the way.*

Luthan was thrown at Emmanuel's feet. Emmanuel looked at his audience. 'An enemy,' he announced. 'One who would have the old ways kept!'

The crowd jeered and someone threw a bottle, which struck Luthan on the back.

'Tell me, Luthan, where are the rest of your people?'
Emmanuel asked, lowering himself down to him.

'I'll tell you,' Luthan hissed. 'But you have something
I want. A key.'

'Ah.' Emmanuel reached under his collar and removed
Felix's key on a cord from round his neck. '*This* key?'

Luthan nodded. 'Give it to me. And I'll tell you
everything.'

'It seems this is rather highly sought after,' Emmanuel
said, and closed his fist round the key. 'I've already been
deceived once, and I don't intend to be again. Take him
away.'

Luthan's hands were bound by the gang. He turned to
Alyn, meeting his eyes and nodding as he was grabbed
under the arms and hauled towards the river. Alyn
looked back at the explosives piled on the grass. *Come
on*, he urged. *Why isn't it working?*

He shut his eyes again, visualizing a blast scattering
Emmanuel's followers. When he opened his eyes a
van appeared from round the corner and sped across
the grass.

'What's Luthan doing?' Elsa whispered, as she and
Jes stood in the crowd. 'They'll kill him!'

She stopped, noticing Emmanuel had removed the
key from round his neck and was dangling it in front of
Luthan, taunting him.

'There it is,' said Jes, not taking her eyes from the key.
'You think you can get him to drop it?'

Elsa shut her eyes and visualized Emmanuel's key landing on the grass at her feet.

She screwed up her face as the pain seared through her skull. The Ability was supposed to work through the imagination, but there was nothing imaginary at all about this pain. Elsa crouched, blood trickling out of her nose, her mind on fire.

'Elsa!'

Jes knelt beside her and put an arm round her shoulders.

'I can't do it, Jes,' Elsa whispered.

Jes looked up to see the van driven by Ryan speeding towards Emmanuel. He leapt out of the way just in time.

The van continued on, moving towards the river at full speed.

'Ryan! Julian!' Jes yelled. 'Get out of there! Jump!'

For a few moments her heart held its beat – until she saw the pair tumbling on to the grass. Then they got up and ran with the crowd of fleeing spectators.

'Stop them!' Emmanuel cried, pointing to Ryan and Julian.

Jes reached into the pocket of her coat and removed a rock. She launched it at Emmanuel, only for it to miss and crash against a tree. She silently cursed.

Alyn watched helplessly as the van crashed through the wall and into the river. A spray of water flew into the air. He looked at the small crate of explosives on the grass.

He shut his eyes again. *It has to work this time*. He imagined the box exploding, throwing Emmanuel and his men over in the blast. A tingling sensation emerged in the back of his mind. He put a hand to his head. His vision became slanted and stretched, as though reality was warping before him. He staggered away before quickly falling to the ground.

Alyn opened his eyes to find one of Emmanuel's men staring at him.

'You!' the man hissed, recognizing Alyn and raising his gun.

Alyn shut his eyes.

At that moment a rock bounced off a tree and hit the man on the side of the head. He fell forward, inadvertently squeezing the rifle trigger. A single burst left the weapon.

The bullet struck the crate of explosives; there was a tremendous blast of sound and heat. Emmanuel's men were thrown through the air and scattered among the smoke and ash.

Ryan swore loudly, leaping out of his skin at the explosion. He pulled Elsa down.

Although they were a short distance away, the force of the blast had thrown Emmanuel to the ground. Ryan watched as a figure sped across the grass.

Alyn.

Alyn reached down and grabbed the key. It had been flung from Emmanuel's hand in the explosion and was lying on a patch of snow.

He stared at it in disbelief for a few moments. Then he turned and saw Jes and Julian some way behind him. 'I've got it!' he yelled. 'It's all over!' He started towards them, but was knocked to the ground by Emmanuel, who was somehow already on his feet.

Emmanuel removed a dagger from his coat pocket. He knelt over Alyn. 'I gave you enough chances, Alyn,' he said. 'You still don't understand. This is what everybody wants! It *has* to happen . . .'

'It's – it's what *you* want,' Alyn spat, watching the blade helplessly.

Emmanuel lifted the dagger, but before he could plunge it into Alyn's chest he was thrown to the side.

Ryan had begun aiming wild punches at him, barely even connecting. Emmanuel tried to shield himself from the blows.

Alyn crawled to his feet. 'Jes!' he yelled, and tossed her the key.

Jes caught it with both hands.

'Come on!' Elsa shouted. 'Get Ryan!'

Alyn grabbed Ryan, trying to pull him from Emmanuel. 'We have to go, Ryan,' he urged. 'Forget about him – we've got what we want. Come on! We have to go!'

Just as he managed to get Ryan into a standing position, there was a rapid cracking burst of gunfire as one of Emmanuel's followers staggered drowsily towards his leader.

'There they are,' Emmanuel snarled, pointing at the pair. 'Kill them both.'

In a silent stupor the man turned his gun at Alyn, who was frozen to the spot.

Ryan threw himself at Alyn, knocking him out of the way.

The weapon rattled for barely a second, but that was all it took. Ryan crumpled softly to the roadside.

Before the man could fire again, Elsa launched a stone at his face. She called out Ryan's name and ran over, followed by Jes.

Jes cried, shaking her head from side to side as she knelt beside him. A pool of blood had already blossomed beneath him. She tried lifting up Ryan's head.

He touched her face gently. 'You've got to help my mum,' he whispered, reaching inside his coat with a trembling hand. He removed Felix's diamond-covered watch. 'Give her this, will you? Say it's a present. From me.' He took a deep breath. 'And tell her I love her.'

'Ryan,' Jes said, but her voice was breaking. 'Please, stay with us.'

'I'm sorry, Jes,' he whispered. 'I – I tried using the Ability . . . on you . . . once . . . to make you like me . . . That's why you kissed me . . . I'm sorry . . .'

Jes pulled him to her. 'No it wasn't,' she said, putting her mouth close to his ear. 'I chose to do that, Ryan.'

Ryan's eyes met hers and for a moment he seemed

completely relieved. Then his eyes remained open, staring serenely at the sky above.

Jes and Elsa both began crying. Julian, who had been watching from afar, was silent and defeated.

Alyn got to his feet. 'Thanks, Ryan,' he said, quietly. 'Thanks.'

He looked round and realized that Emmanuel and his followers were nowhere to be seen. He and his friends were all alone.

57

'He pushed me out of the way,' Alyn eventually said, as he and the others stood together on Bridge Street, just minutes on foot from where Ryan's body lay. They had stayed with him for as long as possible, before Alyn removed his coat and laid it over him and left in silence.

'He saved me.'

Jes nodded. Her eyes had been focused on the same spot on the road. The events of the past few minutes seemed unreal, as though she had watched the entire thing through someone else's eyes.

'I don't know what else to say,' Alyn said. His voice was almost a whisper.

Jes dried her eyes on her sleeve. 'Don't say anything.'

He put his arm round her but she pushed him away.

Beside her, Elsa sat on the road, covering her face with her hands. Julian traced patterns on the pavement with his finger.

Alyn unscrewed the shaft from Felix's key and removed the bit of paper. 'Fifty-one point fifty-one.'

Then he unscrewed the shaft from Stephen's key. 'Seven, seven, one, two.'

Julian unwound the shaft on Blythe's key. 'Minus nought point twelve.'

Only then did Elsa look up. She took Antonia's key and removed the shaft. 'Five, six, nine, eight.'

'Coordinates,' said Julian.

Alyn picked up an overturned dustbin and launched it at the glass door of a tourist shop bedecked with Union Jack flags, T-shirts and posters. He reached through the glass, opened the door and went in. Several minutes later, Alyn returned with a bound map of London. He threw it towards Julian.

Then Alyn picked up the bin and threw it again and again and again at the shop window until the glass trickled out on to the ground in a powder of glittery dust. He began to sob into his hands.

Jes hurried over and put her arms round his shoulders. In each other's arms they swayed from side to side, as though attempting some strange, uncoordinated dance.

Julian looked away from them, then reached down and flicked through the map.

After a short while, he pointed to a grid. 'Here,' he said.

'Museum Street? That's not far from here,' Elsa said, looking over and wiping her nose again.

Julian tore the page out and shoved it in his pocket. 'Jes, Alyn!' he called. 'Let's go.'

58

'Now what?' Elsa said breathlessly as they came to Museum Street almost half an hour later. Rows of little shops were shuttered and boarded along both sides. Apart from a tramp scavenging through a bin on the corner, there was not a soul around.

'This is definitely the right place,' Julian answered, comparing it to the map. 'We just have no idea what we're looking for.'

The group separated and began wandering up and down the street.

Almost twenty minutes passed and they were still none the wiser about what to do next. In his frustration Julian sat on an upturned bin and planted his head in his hands.

'Help us, Julian!' Elsa called over, beckoning him to stand.

'Help you do what? Get even more confused? We don't know what we're looking for!'

Elsa shook her head disappointedly and hurried after Jes and Alyn.

It was as Julian turned his eyes from her that he paused. In front of him was a bookshop.

KRISTOF & PLEDGE
ANTIQUARIAN BOOKS

'I think I've found it,' he said, standing slowly. He waited in the silence for a response from the others that never came. '*I said I think I've found it!*'

Elsa was the first to reach him. She glanced at the shuttered door sceptically, then looked up at the sign.

'Kristof . . . and *Pledge*. This has to be it.'

Alyn took a step towards the door and peered through the shutters. Inside everything was dark. He rang the buzzer.

'No one here,' said Elsa. She leant down and picked up a small stone and launched it at the window.

A dog began barking somewhere in the distance. Moments later, a face appeared at the window on the upper floor.

'What is it?' growled an old man, pushing the window open. He had a round bulb-shaped nose and tufts of grey hair creeping eccentrically out of his skull like weeds.

'We've come for something!' Elsa called up to him.

'We're not open. Now go away.'

The man was about to slam the window shut when Elsa shouted back up to him. 'Please,' she said. 'This is really, *really* important.'

The old man sighed. 'What do you want?'

'We don't know,' Alyn answered. 'But something was left here for us.'

'Felix!' Julian called up. 'James Felix. The billionaire who died recently. Has he ever visited your shop?'

The man paused, squinting down at the group. 'Not Felix, no. But a man came here a year ago and asked if we could store something for Mr Felix in our cabinet. An antique book, I presumed. I thought it was a strange request, young man, but he paid very well, so who was I to turn him down?' He smiled, but his smile quickly turned to suspicion. 'Who are you?'

'We've come to collect that parcel,' Alyn replied.

'Is that so? Do you really think I'm just going to let you have it?'

'How else would we know?' Julian argued. 'And, besides, it *isn't* a book.' He lifted one of the keys. 'It's a machine.'

The old man gave Julian a sceptical look and disappeared from the window. A couple of minutes later he appeared at the door, downstairs.

'Come on then,' said the man, lifting the shutters. He still seemed wary of the group, examining each one of them in turn.

They quickly entered before he changed his mind. The shelves were overflowing with books. The shop smelt of damp paper and cardboard, a welcoming, even intoxicating, scent.

'Come,' the bookseller muttered impatiently.

The group followed him into the next room. The far wall was lined with glass cabinets.

The owner shuffled through the keys on his belt and opened one of the cabinets. Inside was a book-shaped parcel.

He removed the parcel and tore away the brown paper. 'Certainly looks like a book to me.'

'Open it,' said Alyn.

The bookseller gave a weary sigh and lifted the cover.

Inside was a hollowed-out page and a small square metal box, not much bigger than a Rubik's Cube. The box contained four keyholes.

Alyn held out his hand. Jes passed him the four keys.

'Wait,' Elsa protested. 'What if the prison just blows up straight away, with everyone inside?'

'And risk killing a hundred inmates?' Alyn shook his head. 'Felix wasn't a murderer.'

'Let's hope not,' Julian answered.

Alyn hesitated for a moment, then tried each of the keys inside a hole until they all fitted.

'Can someone tell me what's going on?' said the bookseller.

'Nothing's happening,' said Elsa.

'The electromagnetic pulse that caused the blackout stopped everything from working,' Julian said, and looked at Alyn. 'Unless . . .'

'Unless we make it work,' Alyn said. He shut his eyes, imagining a butterfly fluttering inside the machine, stirring the dormant static charge into a tiny electrical surge.

He surrendered to his imagination, watching in a trance as clouds cracked and sizzled, laced with sparks of white like some thunderstorm bringing the end of the world. His eyelids flickered and he felt the warm trickle of blood on his lip. One of the others was calling his name, but the sound was muffled and muted, as though it was underwater.

Alyn opened his eyes. The light on the box began flashing red and beeping, until the beeps and flashes grew into a rapid flicker.

'You did it,' was the last thing he heard. And then nothing.

59

It was the boy at the front of the classroom who first noticed the sound coming out of the speakers. It was little more than a faint crackle, but, if he strained his ears, he was sure he could hear a voice.

He looked around, while the projector light flickered over him. It was getting louder.

'Eyes on the screen,' said the guard, pointing his ibis at him.

The boy raised his hand. 'Sir, there's a sound ... a noise ...'

'I can hear it too,' said a girl at the back of the room.

One of the guards marched along the aisle of desks. 'If you don't shut it right now, I swear I'm going to –'

'*Evacuate immediately,*' boomed the recorded voice from the loudspeaker. '*This facility will destruct in ten minutes. Evacuate immediately ...*' An alarm wailed painfully, echoing off the concrete walls.

A wave of agitation spread among the inmates, and many clambered out of their seats.

'Sit back down!' yelled one of the guards, firing his ibis.

The security light above the classroom door bleeped and there was a metallic click as the door unlocked, as did each of the cells in unison.

'We're free!' one of the inmates shouted, once the clatter of metal had ceased.

At least two guards were knocked to the floor and trampled as the inmates collectively charged for the exit.

Susannah left her office and walked briskly along the corridor. She clutched the folder close to her chest. In it was everything she needed for a new life: a passport, money. *A fresh start.* She could feel Nowhere start to tremble beneath her feet, and dust and plaster broke from the ceiling.

When Susannah turned, a small blond-haired boy was watching her by the door at the far end. A little smear of dried blood was on his upper lip.

'Tom!' Susannah gasped. 'Didn't you hear the evacuation warning? Get a move on, will you?'

Tom remained still.

'Quickly!' Susannah urged. She began running towards the door.

'Guess you were right after all,' he said. 'I am a bad person. I've done awful things . . . I'm guilty.'

With that, he shut the door and locked it, leaving Susannah trapped inside.

'No!' Susannah yelled, running at the door. 'It was all a lie . . . to make you compliant . . . You're not . . . you're not a bad person. None of you are!'

'Aren't I?' she heard him say from the other side of the door.

'Wait,' Susannah begged. 'Please, open it up! Let me out!'

But he had already gone. The scent of brick and dust and rubble filled the air. She turned and ran back along the length of the corridor to the door at the other end but by then it was too late: a crack had appeared in the concrete beneath her feet and everything came apart – the walls, the ceiling and the floor. Susannah had just enough time to take a final breath.

It seemed to take an age before the cloud of dust settled after the explosion. Amid the spluttering and shouting and crying, Henry was leant over by a tree, coughing noisily into his fist.

'Are you – are you gonna tell me what was going on?' a baffled guard asked Henry.

Henry coughed a final time into his hand. Slowly he straightened his back.

'You mean to tell me you had no idea?' he said. 'You've been keeping all these children captive, in a forest, despite them telling you they were all innocent?'

'But they –'

'Despite you all *brainwashing* them? You didn't think to speak out about it? Tell people what had happened?'

'They – they said it was just some ... some new scheme.'

Henry glared at him, disbelieving.

'I – I was just obeying orders,' said the guard, as if to excuse himself.

'Obeying orders,' Henry repeated. 'Just obeying orders.' He shook his head and walked round to the far end of the crowd of over ninety children and ten guards, who were staring at the ruins in disbelief.

'All of you!' Henry shouted, and waited for silence to resume. 'All of you have been part of something that you never should have been. Not just you,' he said, turning from the children to the guards. 'But you too. And now you're going home. You're free.'

He let his words sink in and said, 'There's a road just a few miles away. Once we make it there, my people will be waiting.' With that, he set off through the trecs, followed by the snaking procession of ninety-four inmates in their grey uniforms.

60

Emmanuel stood opposite the abandoned underground station, surrounded by a dozen of his followers with flaming torches. He looked at the man beside him, who was holding a piece of gauze against a cut on his forehead.

'It was here that they attacked me,' the man said. He pointed at the alleyway. 'They came from down there.'

Emmanuel walked down the alleyway. His fingers skimmed the brick.

'They're here,' he murmured. 'I can *feel* the Ability.' He looked over his shoulder. 'I want none of them left alive.'

He stood beside the boarded wooden door and pushed it.

The door creaked open. Emmanuel took a flaming torch from one of the group and held it to the darkness.

'Who's there?' came a weak voice. 'Elsa? Ryan? Is that you?'

Before Emmanuel could place a foot inside, a hand grabbed his arm.

'Sir, look!' said one of his men.

Emmanuel turned to see a street lamp flickering. And then another. Soon the whole row of lights returned to life.

'I thought the power wasn't coming back until we'd –'

'It's over,' Emmanuel said quietly, and was filled with a sudden sense of despair.

As he said this, a cacophony of car alarms, sirens and noise filled the street, a wonderful manic mess of music.

'The police will be here soon,' said one of the men, touching Emmanuel's arm. 'We'd better get going.'

With that, each of the men sprinted out of the alleyway, all except for Emmanuel, who remained motionless. He had been close, this time. Closer than he had ever come before. Another day or two and it might have had a different ending. He waited until the whining sirens were close before he turned and left.

61

As the power seeped back into the city, sirens wailed and alarms clattered and rang, competing like electric birdsong. Jes sat with Alyn's head in her lap on the floor of the bookshop. Realizing his phone was working, the bookseller had dashed upstairs to call for an ambulance.

Elsa appeared at her side. 'Is he still . . . ?'

Jes nodded. 'You guys need to go back to the station. They'll need you.'

'What about you?'

'I'm staying here,' Jes said. 'I'm not leaving him.'

Elsa jogged over to Julian, who was standing outside.

'I don't know if you can hear me,' Jes said, brushing Alyn's hair out of his eyes. 'But we did it. We stopped the Pledge. We stopped Emmanuel. I just –' She held her breath. 'I think we were too late to stop the sickness. I'm sorry, Alyn . . .'

'You weren't too late,' Alyn whispered.

Jes peered down at him. 'Alyn,' she said. 'You're awake.'

'Reality is healing,' he whispered. 'I can feel it. The sickness is going.' He gave her a weak smile. 'We weren't too late.'

62

Three days later

Harlan opened his eyes. Outside his window a branch was moving gently in the wind. He patted his sheet. The cotton felt rough and scratchy beneath his fingertips.

'Harlan,' said his father. He hurried round to the side of his son's bed and clutched his hand.

'Dad?'

'Amina!' he yelled. 'Amina, come here – he's awake!'

Harlan's mother rushed into the room and both of them threw their arms round him. Then Harlan's two brothers appeared and ran over to his bed too. Harlan started laughing and soon they all joined in.

'I don't remember a thing,' Harlan muttered, brushing his hands through his hair. 'How long have I been here?'

'Three days. A strange young woman in a sports car dropped you off.'

'What happened?'

'A psychological episode,' said his father. 'That's what the doctor said. They had no other explanation for it.'

'And don't think I've forgiven you for running away from home,' Harlan's mother scolded. 'You have no idea what you put us through, Harlan.'

'Running away from home ...' Harlan pondered, staring at the beckoning branch outside.

'Yes,' his father said, his eyes burning furiously. 'Unless of course there's something else you want to tell us ... ?'

Harlan shook his head. 'Nothing else ...'

'The young woman said to give this to you,' said his father, handing Harlan an envelope. 'I've got to call the rest of the family; your aunt and uncles will want to see you.'

'Let's give the poor boy some privacy to open his letter,' said his older brother.

Harlan waited until his family had left, then lifted the envelope and tore it open. Inside was a piece of paper.

Harlan,
Guess you're now a full member of the Guild. Give us
a call as soon as you're feeling up to it.
Pyra. X

There was a telephone number jotted below.

'What's in the letter, Harlan?' his mother called from the next room.

Harlan crushed the letter into a ball and tossed it down the side of his bed. He knew there was such a thing as magic; he had seen it, *felt* it. The world was a stranger place than he had ever realized and that was enough. That was all he would ever need.

'Nothing,' he replied, trying to hide a smile. 'Nothing at all.'

63

'Well, I think it suits you,' Elsa said, gazing at Julian's misshapen ear, as the pair walked together through the snowy park.

Julian frowned at her and touched his ear delicately.

'The worst part is no one will ever believe me when I tell them it was bitten off by a psychopathic billionaire who was trying to kill me.' He sighed. 'I'll just have to lie. Then again, I suppose we all will. This whole thing will have to be our secret, won't it?'

He had a point, Elsa thought. Jes had told them about her parents' reaction when she had returned home; how they hadn't believed a word of what she'd said; how they'd thought she'd lost her mind. The funny thing was that Jes was the only one who *hadn't* come close to doing so.

Since destroying the prison the sickness had relinquished its grip and before long they were all back to normal. Well, as normal as they *could* be, anyway. Still, Elsa wasn't keen to try using the Ability for some time.

'Then again ...' Julian smirked. '*You* could always

tell your parents you ran away to join the circus. The world's smallest clown.'

'I've missed you being mean to me, Julian,' she answered with a satisfied sigh.

She spotted a couple of teenagers throwing snowballs at each other nearby. She shut her eyes.

Moments later, one of them raised a snowball but slipped on a patch of ice. The snowball sailed out of her hand and hit Julian in the face.

Julian gasped, wiping the snow away with his sleeve. He looked at Elsa indignantly, but she gave an innocent smile.

One last time won't hurt, she thought.

A short distance from Julian and Elsa, Jes and Alyn sat in Trafalgar Square together. Pigeons pecked around their feet, while groups of tourists flocked around the fountain, taking photographs.

'When are you going home?' he asked, turning to her.

Jes shrugged. 'I want to go to Ryan's house. Speak to his mum.' She removed the watch from her pocket. 'Give her this. Just like Ryan wanted.'

'So soon? You think that's a good idea?'

Jes scooped up some crumbs from inside her cardboard sandwich box and tossed them to the pigeons. They immediately charged for the crumbs, fighting each other.

'Jes? I said –'

She shrugged, not answering the question. 'So what are you going to do? Aren't you going back home?'

Alyn shook his head. 'I don't really have one. There's nothing for me back there.'

She touched his arm. 'I'm sure the Guild would look out for you.'

He nodded. It was a possibility. Ever since Emmanuel's defeat, he couldn't shake the feeling of melancholy. Everything had gone back to the way it was, but why did it all seem so peculiar – so *hollow*?

'You ever wonder what things might be like if Emmanuel had won?'

'He didn't win, Alyn.' Jes touched his face and kissed his cheek. 'We did. We won.'

He looked at her, smiled and squeezed her hand tight. Jes leant her head against his shoulder and closed her eyes. Alyn stared into the distance, watching the traffic streaming past.

Epilogue

'Mind if I sit?' said the man in the black overcoat, gesturing to a bar stool.

The man nearby sighed, loosening his collar. 'Be my guest.'

'Rough day?'

'Could say that.' He forced a smile. 'Don't know how they expect anyone to cope any more. I've had to lay off three staff . . . Times are hard, you know. And the government? They just don't care about us small businesses any more. They only care about the corporations.'

The figure opposite him nodded sympathetically. 'Sometimes I think we'd be better off without governments altogether.'

'You're not the only one, pal. Lots of people are angry, you know. Seems like there's a fuse, just waiting to be lit . . . Remember all the stuff that happened in London, years ago?'

The man in the black overcoat nodded. The faintest smile emerged on his lips. 'I remember it well. I was there.' He stopped talking for a moment, then said, 'What if I told you I had a method of making you rich, richer than you ever thought was possible?'

'I'd say what's the catch?'

The man smiled. 'No catch. In fact, we could use this method to . . . to change things for the better.'

'You mean like magic?'

'Yes. In a sense.'

'Look, I'm not the type to believe in that kinda stuff. I'm gonna need some proof before I –'

The lights in the bar flickered briefly before suddenly extinguishing and plunging the room into darkness.

There was a moment's silence before the man began laughing hysterically.

'Friend,' he replied, shaking his head in disbelief. 'You've got a deal.'

Acknowledgements

Thanks so much to everyone who has helped out along the way: Claire Wilson, Lexi Hamblin and RCW; Shannon Cullen, Ben Horslen, Laura Squire, Wendy Shakespeare, Katy Finch, Matt Jones, Tania Vian-Smith, Nicola Chapman, Jessica Farrugia-Sharples and everyone else at Penguin Random House; Bella Pearson; and to anyone else who has helped on a practical, editorial or promotional level. Huge thanks to the YouTubers and bloggers who have said nice things about the books; to Shelley Lee for all of the bookings; and to all the schools and students I've visited over the past few years. Thanks also to my friends; mum, Christine; the Courtney family; and of course Sarah.